Skeletons & Scandals

Confessions of a Closet Medium
Book 10

Nyx Halliwell

Beach
Path
Publishing
LLC

Skeletons & Scandals, Confessions of a Closet Medium, Book 10

©2025 Nyx Halliwell

ISBN: 978-1-964028-26-2

Cover Art by Fanderclai Design www.fanderclai.com

Formatting by Beach Path Publishing, LLC

Prologue

Previously, in Phantoms Are Forever...

Following Persephone and Tabby, I climb to the second floor and look up when Persephone points at the attic steps. "What is it?" I ask.

"I've just been made aware of a situation that we need to handle," she says, without a lick of sarcasm or pushiness in her voice.

If anything, her lack of emotion makes me wary. "A situation in my attic?"

I find myself following her and the cat into the dark, dusty third floor. Night has fallen, and I flip on the single light that hangs from the rafters. It throws layers of shadows over the collection of furniture, trunks, and discarded boxes of belongings that I've never found time to sort through.

Tabby hops over stacks of books, magazines, and newspapers, then weaves behind a dress form and a wooden rocking chair. She perches on top of a chest with metal hinges and leather buckles.

Persephone juts her chin. "Open it."

It's not as easy for me to get to it as it was for the cat. "I could use a flashlight."

"You won't need it in a minute," my guardian angel says.

A chill slides over my shoulder. "Just tell me what's inside that's so important."

She shakes her head. "This is one of those times when I can't say anything. All I can do is point you in the right direction."

The chill curls around my spine. I have to move the dress form out of the way and I sneeze from the dust from the newspaper stacks as I relocate them as well. I finally make it to the chest, and Tabby jumps down.

"I'm not going to like this, am I?"

Neither of them replies, and I reach for any kind of psychic message that might come through to warn me before I lift the lid. I'm not like Kit, Sage, or my aunt. There's a lot going on inside my brain, and I'm imagining a storm of unnerving things that could be happening.

Best to get it over with.

The leather straps are worn and closed like a belt buckle. I wrestle with the tight material to release the clasp, then brush the dust from my hands. "Okay," I say, dragging up as much courage as I can. "Let's see what secrets you're hiding."

Of all the things I thought my aunt might have stored in this chest, what I see is not one of them.

At first, I think my eyes are deceiving me. Or that maybe it's a Halloween prop.

The smell that emanates from the chest tells me differently. I cover my nose and mouth with a hand, partly to shut out the odor and partly to hold in my cry of disbelief. My shadow falls over the contents, and I shift, trying to get more illumination on them. Unfortunately, that doesn't help.

It's no prop.

What I'm looking at inside Aunt Willa's trunk is a...

"This has to be a trick," I say. "A mistake."

"It's not," Persephone argues. "A scandal, yes. You have quite a mystery to figure out, Ava, and it looks like your aunt has something to answer for."

Blank, bottomless eye sockets stare back at me. Below them, a set of teeth seem to grimace.

This is so much worse than anything I'd imagined.

Locked away in this abandoned trunk in my attic is a human skeleton.

Chapter One

"Logan! Logan, you need to get up here right now!" My voice bounces off the sloped attic ceiling, sending dust motes dancing through the beams of afternoon sun. I can't tear my eyes away from what's nestled in Aunt Willa's antique trunk.

A skeleton. A human skeleton, curled up as if trying to fit inside before someone slammed the lid shut.

I hear Logan's footsteps on the stairs, his breath catching as he reaches the last step. "Ava? What is it?"

His normally composed lawyer face drops completely as he steps beside me. His mouth hangs open just long enough for a dust bunny to consider moving in.

"Is that what I think it is?" he whispers, his tanned face paling.

"Unless Aunt Willa had a surprisingly realistic Halloween decoration that nobody ever mentioned? Yeah, it's exactly what you think it is." I fold my arms, partly from the chill suddenly taking over the attic and partly because I don't know what else to do with my hands.

Persephone has conveniently disappeared.

Logan runs his fingers through his already tousled hair and kneels beside the trunk. The wood floor creaks beneath his weight as he leans forward. "The bones are aged," he murmurs. "Whoever this was has been here a long time. Decades, maybe."

"In my aunt's trunk. In my attic." The implications settle heavily in my stomach. "This is bad."

Logan's eyes narrow as he studies the trunk's hinges and worn leather straps. His fingers trace the edge, and he picks up a metal shape from the floor. A rusted lock. "Was this on it?"

I shrug. "I have no idea."

"The trunk itself looks like it's from the 1950s." He points to some faded inscriptions on the inside of the lid, then peers into the corners. "There are no clothes, no jewelry. The simple size of the skeleton, though, suggests someone on the petite side."

Lawyer-mode activated. "Are you playing detective? Your specialty is family law, not skeletal law." I'm aiming for humor, but my voice comes out higher than intended.

He glances up with that half-smile that makes my heart skip. His expression sobers quickly, though, when he sees my dismay. "I'm certainly no expert. We need to call—"

"The police," I finish for him, already feeling a headache forming behind my eyes. "Detective Jones is going to love this. He already thinks I'm the freak who talks to ghosts."

"You *do* talk to ghosts," Logan reminds me gently, standing up and brushing dust from his khakis. "But this time, you didn't need your ability to find trouble. It was waiting right here in this trunk. Any idea where it came from?"

I look down at the skeleton again, at the curved spine and the delicate finger bones. Female, I think to myself, like he said. "No clue." Who was she? How did she end up forgotten in an attic trunk that now belongs to me? "Aunt Willa," I whisper to the rafters, "a little warning would have been nice."

A meow draws my attention. Tabby, my witchy shifter, many-times removed grandmother in feline form, twitches her whiskers at me. At least she's not in her human form naked, as she so often likes to galivant around.

"Tabby, no!" I start, but it's too late. Cats and boundaries have never been on speaking terms.

She hops right in with the skeleton, ignoring my protests. Her golden eyes narrow as she sniffs around the ribcage.

"Logan, get her away from there." I wave my hands. "That's evidence. Or remains. Or...something!"

Logan makes a dismissive gesture. "You know how well that works. She's her own woman."

Can't argue with that. "So am I, but...ugh!" I throw up my hands as Tabby's attention intensifies. She extends a dainty orange paw beneath the bony fingers of the skeleton's right hand. Something glints in the dim light.

"What is she doing?" I whisper, moving closer against my better judgment.

Tabby lets out a triumphant meow and hooks her claws around something metallic, dragging it into view. I squint, our shadows keeping it in the dark.

But seeing it sends a jolt through me. The attic air feels

stifling. I lift out a small, dented tin box no bigger than a deck of cards.

"Don't open it," Logan warns. "And you should wear gloves. Detective Jones will have our hides if we tamper with evidence. He'll never let me hear the end of it."

"Evidence?" I place the tin on a nearby dresser. "Of what, exactly? You think it's tied to the skeleton?"

He pulls his phone out of his pocket, hesitates, then makes the call we both dread. "We don't know, so it's better to err on the side of caution."

"Please tell him this isn't my fault." The dread pervades my entire system. "I didn't murder anyone. I just found their remains. In our attic. That I inherited. From my aunt. Who apparently collected more than teacups and questionable quilts."

Logan steps to the far corner of the attic, punching in Jones's number with a resigned expression. I hear the rumble of his voice explaining the situation with the kind of calm that makes him so effective in a courtroom. Too calm, if you ask me.

Tabby purrs, looking supremely satisfied with her detective work. "Check your pride, grandmother," I whisper to her. "This could end badly for all of us."

She flicks her tail and pads off downstairs. Logan returns, slipping his phone into his pocket. His expression tells me everything I need to know. And his deep sigh? The prelude to exasperated sarcasm. "Jones is thrilled, I take it?"

He said, and I quote, 'Of course it's Fantome. Why would it be anyone else? She's a magnet for the weird.' Then he asked if you'd communed with the skeleton's ghost yet."

I roll my eyes. "Classic."

Logan's lips twitch in amusement. "He's on his way with Dr. Abernathy. The county ME is off for the weekend, so Doc is filling in. He said not to touch anything and, specifically, to 'make sure your wife doesn't start a séance before I get there.'"

"That's Kit and Sage's area of expertise. The ghosts just show up for me. It's not like I send invitations. If I did, they'd all RSVP with unfinished business."

Logan drapes an arm around my shoulders. "What does your sixth sense tell you about this one?"

I look at the skeleton, at the tin, at the trunk that's been sitting innocently in my aunt's attic for who knows how long. "That Detective Jones is right about one thing," I sigh. "I'm a magnet for the weird. Why is it always me?"

The air in the attic shifts, as if someone has opened a window on the other side of the room. I glance toward the single dormer window, but it's tightly latched. Logan doesn't seem to notice, his focus fixed on the trunk.

"You feel that?" I ask, my voice barely above a whisper.

Logan glances around. "No, what?"

That's when I see her—or rather, through her. A woman appears near the trunk, her form flickering and jerky like footage from an old film reel. She wears a sleeveless blouse tucked into cigarette pants with an apron tied around her waist. Her hair is swept up in a messy bun of dark, ringlet-like curls.

"Oh," I breathe, my heartbeat quickening. "Hello there."

Logan's head swivels toward the trunk. "The ghost?"

The woman's eyes widen in surprise, fear, or maybe relief? Her body flickers between translucence and a more substantial form. Her mouth moves, but I hear nothing.

"I'm so sorry, I can't understand you," I tell her. "But I can see you. These are your remains, aren't they?"

Logan stays silent, watching me with the patient expression he's perfected since discovering my peculiar talent. The ghost points toward the tin, then toward me, urgency in her gesture.

"The tin means something to you. Can you show me—"

Her form flickers violently. My chest feels a tug, a wrenching. She stretches, contracts, then disperses into nothing more than a faint shimmer.

"Wait!" I reach for her. "Don't go!"

"And...she's gone, isn't she?" Logan asks.

I nod, disappointment settling over me. "She was trying to tell me something about the tin. I need to find out what it was."

The creak of the stairs beneath us interrupts any further speculation. Heavy, measured footsteps announce Detective Jones's arrival long before he appears, slightly winded from the climb.

"Fantome." He gives a curt nod, his bushy eyebrows drawn together in his permanent expression. "Already started the ghost whispering, I see."

Here we go. "Good evening to you, too, Detective. "How's your blood pressure? Those stairs are mighty steep."

Jones grunts, his gaze shifting from me to the trunk. Behind him, Dr. Abernathy ascends the stairs with more grace. "Miss Ava." His voice is warm and reassuring. "What a predicament you've found yourself in. Though I must say, your aunt would have found this entire situation terribly interesting. A mystery to be solved."

Logan and I have to squeeze ourselves between several

stacks of boxes as Jones moves toward the trunk, each wooden plank protesting under his weight. In contrast, Dr. Abernathy's footfalls are nearly silent as he follows, adjusting his round spectacles. The sudden silence makes me jumpier than the creaking did.

"We need more light." Jones pulls on latex gloves. "Got anything brighter?"

Logan turns on his phone's flashlight. "Best I can do unless you want me to grab some lamps."

"This is fine for now," Jones grunts. He snaps pictures and records video, noting the day, time, and location.

Once he's done, he awkwardly moves aside so Dr. Abernathy can examine the skeleton. "Fascinating," Doc murmurs. "There are no clothes or other markers to identify it."

Jones makes notes in his spiral pad. "Any guess on how old it is?"

"How old was the victim, or how long has the body been in the trunk?" Doc shakes out a black body bag and unzips it. "Can't speak to either until I do a full autopsy."

I flinch at the sound of the zipper. Jones grunts and turns to me. "And you saw its ghost, I presume?"

I cross my arms. "As a matter of fact, yes. Just before you arrived."

"Of course you did." I swear he practices this tone in the mirror. "And what did this ghost tell you?"

"She tried to communicate, but she vanished before she could."

"I see," Jones mumbles, making another note.

I catch Logan's eye, and he gives me a subtle wink. The

detective might not believe in my abilities, but at least my husband is in my corner.

Jones moves around the cramped attic space and gestures at the stairs. "Let's continue this conversation downstairs. Dr. Abernathy needs space to work."

"Perhaps Logan would stay and assist?" Doc asks.

I glance once more at the trunk before following Jones. Logan gives my hand a quick squeeze, offering silent support as I pass.

The living room seems too bright after the attic's dimness. Jones points at the sofa for me to sit like I'm a suspect in his interrogation room.

"So," he begins, notepad at the ready. "Where exactly did this trunk come from?"

"I honestly don't know." I settle into the cushions, petting Moxley, Logan's basset hound, behind the ears. "It was already in the house when I inherited everything from Aunt Willa. I haven't gone through much of anything up there yet."

"You expect me to believe you've owned this house for nearly two years and never once checked the attic?"

"Have you seen my to-do list?" Heat rises in my cheeks. "Moving home, taking over Aunt Willa's event planning business, starting my wedding gown business, and getting married took up a lot of my time. The attic wasn't exactly priority number one."

"And all your ghost-whispering antics. Seems like they keep you busy."

"You don't have to believe in my abilities, Detective. The ghosts don't care either way." I straighten my spine, channeling Aunt Willa's dignified posture. "But I'd appreciate it if you'd focus on the actual skeleton in my attic rather than my ability to see spirits."

Jones snorts. "Did your special ghost powers give you any insights about our victim?"

I count to three silently. "As I mentioned, she appeared briefly but vanished before communication was established. She seemed confused. Maybe scared." I leave off the part about her reaching for the tin. If he wants to be rude, I'll just keep that to myself, and that tin is going to help me connect with her, I'm sure of it.

Besides, I'm dying to look inside.

"And you have no recollection of your aunt ever mentioning this trunk? No stories about it?"

"None. Aunt Willa kept plenty of secrets, but hiding a body seems a bit extreme, even for her."

"People surprise you," Jones says flatly. "Even the ones you think you know."

The stairs creak, and we both turn to watch Dr. Abernathy come down with Logan, carrying the body bag. The careful way they move makes my throat tighten—this was once a person, and she was trapped in the trunk quite possibly for decades.

"We've secured the remains, Detective." Dr. Abernathy's voice maintains that gentle bedside manner even when discussing a skeleton. He turns to me, his round spectacles catching the light. "Miss Ava, I'll take the utmost care with your...unexpected guest. Rest assured, she'll be treated with dignity. Everyone deserves that in the end, no matter how they came to be forgotten."

"Thank you, Doc."

Jones clears his throat. "I'll need that preliminary report as soon as possible."

"Of course, of course," Dr. Abernathy nods. "Though some things shouldn't be rushed. Death has already claimed all the time this poor soul had—we can spare a little of ours to do things properly."

With a respectful nod toward me, Doc moves toward the door. Logan helps him navigate the body bag through the entryway, and I watch as they carefully load it into the ME's vehicle. An officer that Jones has called arrives, and the two of them wrap up the trunk and haul it out as evidence.

As I watch them all drive away, I pray the ghost comes back and tells me what happened to her.

Chapter Two

Before I can turn for the living room, Brax and Rhys, who run the B&B next door, enter through the back porch and emerge from the kitchen.

"My word." Rhys' eyes are wide in his freckled face. He's dressed in gray sweatpants and a yellow tank top, and he's fanning himself. "What happened over here?"

Brax's concern causes a wrinkle between his brows. He's less casual, wearing black slacks and a purple button-down. "Are you okay?"

Before I can answer, my mother throws open the front door, a hurricane in a tailored pantsuit. "Avalon Fantome! What is this about a body in your house?" Mama's graying blond curls bounce with indignation as she strides in, my father Nash trailing behind with an apologetic smile.

"Hello to you, too, Mama." I accept her perfunctory cheek kiss, the scent of her Chanel No. 5 perfume engulfing me. "This news traveled fast, even for Thornhollow."

"Brax called me the moment he saw the police pull up."

15

Of course he did. Small-town grapevines are faster than Wi-Fi.

Mama brushes imaginary lint from my shoulder. "And Doc was here, too?"

Daddy wraps me in a bear hug. "You okay, sweetheart?"

"I'm fine." I collapse onto the sofa, waving at all of them to make themselves at home. "But finding skeletal remains in your attic isn't exactly in the homeowner's manual."

Mama perches on the edge of an armchair and blinks. "You found *what*?"

Brax and Rhys pour wine as I launch into what led me upstairs in the first place. Logan returns as I'm filling them in about the ghost woman who was attached to the bones. Mama's perfectly plucked eyebrows climb higher with each detail.

"And the trunk was just...up there?" Daddy points at the ceiling.

"I had no idea it existed until today." I look pointedly at Mama. "Any chance you know how Aunt Willa came to have an antique trunk with a skeleton in her attic?"

Mama waves her hand dismissively. "I remember that old thing. Ugly as a wet cat in a bonnet. Goodness, Ava, it's just a prop. She bought it ages ago."

"A prop?" Logan and I say in unison.

"For the display windows." Mama waves that hand again, this time at the front of the house. My cats, Arthur and Lancelot, are occupying said windows, unconcerned with the hubbub. "Willa loved it for the vintage charm, especially when she did her Victorian dress displays, complete with lace gloves and feathered hats. Every year when she used it, someone would offer to buy it from her."

I try to process this. "You're saying Aunt Willa knowingly displayed a trunk with human remains in her shop window?"

Rhys puts a hand to his mouth. "Good Lord."

"Don't be ridiculous," Mama scolds. "She had no idea what was in it."

Logan sets down his wine glass untouched. "She never opened it?"

"She couldn't." Mama sits farther back in the chair. "It had a rusty iron lock on it and no one had the key."

"Where did she get it?" I ask.

Mama's fingers tap her knee while she thinks. "Some estate sale, I think. Must have been... twenty-five, thirty years ago?"

How many skeletons are hiding in Thornhollow's estate sales?

Logan leans forward. "Do you remember whose estate?"

"Heavens, no." The tapping increases as she mentally flips through memories like index cards. "It might have been the Blackwoods? No, no." She glances at Daddy. "Was it that peculiar house on Magnolia Drive? I think she got it right before Ava was born..."

Daddy shrugs, giving me an apologetic look. "Can't say I remember anything about it."

Pressure is building behind my eyes. I rub them. "That's not helpful."

"Well, I'm sorry." Mama straightens her jacket, looking put out. "It wasn't as if I didn't have a few things on my mind at the time, being pregnant with you and all."

"I didn't mean it that way, Mama." I heave a sigh. "It's been a shock, is all."

Logan rubs my arm. "All we know is that we have a mystery skeleton that came from a mystery estate sale three decades ago."

Brax, who's standing with an arm on the mantel of the fireplace, lets out a soft whistle. "Detective Jones is going to love that."

Logan shrugs. "Doc will figure out who the woman was, and we'll go from there."

"Why is Doc doing the autopsy?" Rhys asks.

"The medical examiner is out of town for the weekend," I tell him. "Doc is filling in."

"I'm sure the trunk was empty when Willa bought it." Mama fidgets. "If there had been a dead body in it, how would she have lifted it? I mean, she wasn't exactly bench pressing such things, even in her prime."

"She probably had Saddler move it," Daddy says.

My uncle Saddler died when I was six. I barely remember him, but he came alive for me in Aunt Willa's stories. He'd been a carpenter and had built the bookshelves in all the rooms of this house as well as the rocking chairs on the front porch. I still have the cedar chest he made for me in the bedroom Logan and I claimed.

Brax toys with his wine glass. "Someone could have added the remains after it was here."

The idea sends a shiver through me. "Someone used this house as a dumping ground for a body?"

Rhys sucks in a scandalous breath. "Or your aunt wasn't as innocent as we all thought."

Everyone freezes. Mama's head snaps up. "You watch your mouth, young man." She gives him the *don't be ridiculous* scowl. "My sister never harmed so much as a stray cat."

I notice how Mama carefully doesn't meet my eyes. There's something she's not saying, but pushing will only make her clam up tighter. That's the thing about Southern mothers—they've elevated withholding information to an art form, all while smiling and offering you sweet tea.

I down a gulp of wine. "Of course she didn't kill anyone. But someone put that woman in that trunk, and now her ghost is wandering around."

Mama stands, smoothing out invisible wrinkles from her pants. "Well, I'm just grateful you found the poor soul. Maybe now she can rest in peace, whoever she is."

The gentleness in her voice is in direct contrast to her commanding presence. Behind the mayor's polished exterior and the bossy mother persona, there are glimpses of the compassionate woman who taught me to leave food out for strays and always help neighbors in need.

She and Daddy kiss my cheeks, and I rise to see them out. Mama pauses at the doorway, her fingers fidgeting with the pearl necklace she always wears to town meetings. "There's something else," she says.

I brace myself. I knew it. "About the trunk?"

A shake of her head. "The Southern Spirits Cookoff is Saturday." She says this as if it's a national emergency, which, in Thornhollow, it practically is.

"And?" I prompt, confused at the change in topic.

"Finding a skeleton in your attic is going to be all over town." Mama's perfectly manicured nails straighten my necklace. "This is terrible timing. Absolutely *dreadful*."

Really? That's what's on her mind? "I'm sorry my discovery of human remains has inconvenienced the town's foodies, Mama."

"Ava," she admonishes in her classic *you are testing my patience* tone, "this isn't about the foodies. It's about civic duty. The cookoff brings in tourism dollars, and the proceeds from this year's event are going to The Birdie House."

The Birdie House is a women's center that supports new mothers who lack family or financial resources. It's named after local legend Birdie Birmingham, a once-renowned Southern cook and folklore icon who vanished without a trace back in the sixties. Since the money will go to help mothers, the cookoff has been rescheduled from later in the year to Mother's Day weekend.

"What does this have to do with me?" Even as I ask, I know. I feel it coming like a summer storm.

Mama squares her shoulders, Mayor Dixie Fantome now fully present. "Margie Raynor's daughter is taking her on a cruise for Mother's Day. She can't judge this year."

"Mama, no—"

"You have to step in."

I look to Daddy for help, but he's suddenly very interested in the wedding dress in the nearest window display.

"I can't judge a cooking contest!" My voice rises an octave. "I burn microwave popcorn. Plus, there's a literal murder investigation happening in my house!"

"It's hardly an investigation." Mama dismisses that notion with a wave of her hand. "And you don't need to know how to cook to appreciate good food. Besides, you're a Fantome—Thornhollow's founding family has always had a place on the judging panel."

"There's only been one previous panel, Mama, and none of our family was on it."

She arches a delicate brow. "Your cousin Stanley was a judge."

"Stanley is my cousin five times removed! And if he's doing it this year, then the founding family is once more represented."

"He can't. It's a rotating position to be sure no one person ends up skewing the results through favoritism."

Don't try to outsmart Dixie Fantome with her own logic. You'll lose every time.

I close my eyes, counting to ten. "Mama, I have a ghost to help, and Detective Jones breathing down my neck. The last thing I need is to be at a public event tasting moonshine-infused peach cobbler."

"Don't be overly dramatic." I nearly laugh at this, coming from the Drama Queen herself. "That's exactly what you need." She rests her hand on my shoulder. "Honey, if you don't show up, people will talk. They'll claim you're hiding something. You know how this town works. They'll suggest you know more about that skeleton than you're letting on."

I blink, realization dawning. "You're worried about how this affects your upcoming reelection."

Something flickers across her face—hurt, maybe—before her mother mask slips back on. "I'm worried about you. Small towns have long memories. If you don't act innocent and show them you're confident, they'll never let you forget it."

Confident about what? That I'm not a killer? That my beloved aunt wasn't?

The worst part is, she's right. I've spent years away from Thornhollow, and coming back with my 'special abilities' has folks whispering. Hiding away might only feed the rumor mill.

"It's only a few hours of your time," she presses. "I already checked with Rosie, and she told me she and Jenn can handle Saturday's wedding. All you need to do is be at the fairgrounds, smile, eat some delicious food, and show everyone that finding a skeleton in your attic is no big deal."

"It *is* a big deal, Mama."

"One that Landon and your father"—she grabs Daddy's arm and yanks him over to us—"will handle."

My father used to work on the Thornhollow police force. He and Landon Jones were partners for a time before he left the force, left town, and pursued his real love—music. He offers a consoling smile. "There isn't much you can do when it comes to the investigation, and your mother's right—I'll help Landon figure it out." He kisses my forehead. "You don't worry, now, y'hear?"

I glance at Logan as he joins us. He shrugs sympathetically.

"Fine." I sigh, the word feeling like surrender. "I'll do it."

Mama's face brightens. "That's my girl! The committee meets tomorrow at five. Wear something nice. Not black," she adds. "Something cheerful. Yellow, maybe. Ask Brax to help you pick something, okay? I'll text you the details."

As she takes Daddy's hand, I catch a glimpse of real relief in her eyes, and beneath my irritation, I feel a tug of affection. For all her manipulations and social maneuvering, Mama is fighting for her town the only way she knows how. And somewhere along the way, I became a soldier in her civic battles. "You're a good girl, Ava," she whispers with a wink.

For a moment, I'm eight years old again, desperate for her approval. "Don't push it," I mutter.

After they leave, I sink onto the sofa. Logan sits beside me, his shoulder a comforting presence against mine. Rhys and Brax are deep in a whispered conversation at the fireplace.

Logan pats my leg. "You know, you don't have to do everything she says."

"Mama's like a hurricane. You can't fight her. You just try to survive."

"And yet you love her anyway."

It's true. For all her faults and all her pushing, Dixie Fantome loves this town and her family with ferocious devotion.

And whether I like it or not, I'm my mother's daughter.

Chapter Three

Logan refills my wine glass. Rhys and Brax halt their conversation and face us with expectation. Moxley curls up at our feet, his droopy eyes watching with canine interest.

I sip my wine. "I can't believe Aunt Willa, had a skeleton in the attic for who knows how long."

"Things are never dull around here," Rhys says.

Tabby makes an entrance, hopping up on the shelf where I have set the tin. She paws it, knocking it to the floor.

"What's that?" Brax asks.

Logan raises both brows, setting down his glass. "You didn't give that to Detective Jones?"

"I know I should have, but he was being rude and I wanted a chance to examine it first. When I saw the woman's ghost, she reached for it. It has significance to her."

Logan uses his lawyer voice. "Because it could be evidence associated with her death. Don't touch it. There might be fingerprints or other DNA that could help us identify her."

I mentally roll my eyes, but he's right. Setting my glass aside, I grab a pair of gardening gloves hanging by the back door, and return with them on. "I just want to have a look, and then I'll turn it over to our dear detective."

Tabby preens next to the fallen tin. It's a pretty thing, even though the pink paint has faded to a peach color. Retrieving it, I return to the couch, turning it over in my hands. Flecks of rust dot its edges like freckles. There's a small latch to keep it closed. I hesitate a moment, my curiosity mingling with nervousness. "Let's see what Tabby uncovered."

I take a deep breath and pry open the latch, which releases with a protesting creak. The scent of aged paper and something herbal wafts up—rosemary, perhaps, or thyme.

"Cards," Logan says, leaning closer.

Rhys and Brax hover over our shoulders, peering in. Tabby hops up on the back of the sofa, placing her front paws on my shoulder.

"Recipe cards," I clarify, lifting out the top one. The paper is yellowed but remarkably well-preserved. Each card is hand-printed in steady block letters. "This one is for Whispering Pimento Cheese Dip. Mama would love that one."

Rhys points to the corner of the card. "What's that?"

"Some kind of sparrow, maybe?" I squint at the delicate bird illustration drawn in faded blue ink. Each of the next cards I examine has a similar bird. "It's on all of them."

Logan squints at the of the titles. "'Clarity Tea—for when the veil must be thinned.' That doesn't sound like your average sweet tea recipe."

"This one is 'Memory Preservation Tincture.'" I flip to another. "And here's 'Binding Cordial to keep secrets where

25

they belong.'" I hesitate, but the next one seems normal. Sort of. "'Back-from-the-Dead BBQ Ribs.'"

Rhys plucks it from my hand. "I'm so going to make this!"

Brax nudges him. "You're getting your fingerprints on it."

"Oh, right." He uses his shirt to wipe off the card and drops it into the growing pile on the coffee table. "I need a copy of that one."

"These aren't your normal recipes for the dinner table." Logan frowns. "They're more like... I don't know what."

"Recipes from the other side," Brax states with a hint of humor.

None of us laughs.

Moxley shakes his head, ears flopping around, and Logan pets him. "I assume they belonged to our attic tenant. Seems odd that they ended up in that trunk with her, though."

Rhys takes the seat Mama vacated. "Oh, sugar, people will kill for a good Southern recipe handed down through generations of family."

The ghost's shimmering form flashes in my memory—her indistinct features, the desperation in her eyes. "She tried to tell me something," I say, more to myself than to the others. "About these. They must have something to do with her death."

Logan is never dismissive about my connection to the supernatural, the way Detective Jones is. He squeezes my hand. "If anyone can figure it out, it's you."

I shuffle through more cards: Protection Brew, Truth-Speaker's Tonic, Forget-Me-Not Elixir. Rest in Peach Cobbler. The recipes call for ordinary ingredients, but include comments in the instructions that you wouldn't typically find in a standard cookbook. More notes dot the margins. When I flip them over, some of the notes read like ghost stories.

"*Mabel Lou Jenkins died in 1952,*" I read out loud, "*but her ghost never left the kitchen at the Magnolia County Inn. No one dared touch her cast iron pot—until Ellen needed a recipe to please a visiting ghost chef. Mabel finally appeared, flour-dusted and fuming, and insisted on supervising the prep of her signature macaroni and cheese. The secret? A cheddar-crunch crust and a whisper of sage.*"

"Sage!" Rhys claps his hands. "My word, that would be delicious."

I push back our glasses and the wine bottle to make more room. I arrange the cards in a fan across the top. "Whoever our ghost is, she considered these dear."

Rhys retrieves a pencil from Rosie's desk and uses it to push the cards around into groups. "'Blackberry Bewitchment Mocktail,' 'Ghost Beans—a.k.a. Baked Beans with Spirit', 'Spirit-Soaked Cornbread Sticks...'" He separates those from the others. "I'm going to need copies of all of these."

"Maybe you should be entering the cookoff with one of these recipes, rather than judging it," Logan teases me.

I laugh. "Good Lord, that would be a disaster. I burn toast."

"You're judging the cookoff?" Brax asks.

"I've been cornered by a very determined Southern lady wielding guilt like a weapon," I admit.

"Mama will be thrilled," he says. Queenie LeFleur is the town's best chef and runs The Beehive Diner. Her meals are to die for, and she's my mother's best friend. "I don't suppose I can bribe you to choose my entry, can I?"

This could get tricky. "You're entering the contest?"

He smiles proudly. "With my famous cornbread casserole."

Rhys leans forward and whispers, "It's delicious, and not only because I told him to add honey to the mix."

Brax playfully bats his arm. "I'm not going to end up disqualified because you're my best friend, am I?"

I have no idea what the rules are. "I'll check with Mama, but I can't imagine it will be a problem."

It's *definitely* a problem. Maybe one that could get me out of being a judge.

I put a pin in that idea, hoping that when I tell Mama it might raise eyebrows—especially if I honestly think Brax's casserole is the best—she'll agree that I find a replacement.

I hold up a card labeled 'Poltergeist Pumpkin Bars.' "These actually sound delicious."

Rhys motions at it. "I'll need that one, too."

"I wonder if you're right, Rhys. That these recipes might have been worth killing for." I sigh. "I mean, I'm assuming she didn't die of natural causes and simply fall into that trunk."

"Then why didn't the killer steal them?" he asks.

Logan looks thoughtful but reluctant when he glances at me. "We really have to give these to Jones."

"Tomorrow," I say, suddenly protective of the tin and its contents. "Tonight, I want to try to connect with the ghost again using them." I pick up a card labeled 'Lavender Lemonade for Lingering Spirits' and feel a tingle in my fingertips. It skates up my arm, and I glance around quickly, hoping case our cook will appear.

She doesn't.

"Are we doing a séance?" Rhys asks with far too much enthusiasm.

"Nothing that radical." Not yet, anyway, but I do want to talk to my friends Sage and Kit to see if they have any thoughts about my mysterious cook. "I think our ghost has been waiting a long time for someone to listen to her and give her peace."

And it looks like I'm the one to do it.

Chapter Four

In Thornhollow, you can count on three things: strong coffee, all the gossip, and good Southern manners. *Mostly* good, anyway.

Overnight, I conduct a thorough search of the recipes online, but come up with nothing. Same for the names listed in the ghost stories. I'm baffled, but call on the historical society and my favorite librarian to search archives for clues while I use one of the recipes.

I make rosemary-tinged Clarity Quiche for breakfast. The entire time, ingredients slide around on the counter, and the cats stay out of the kitchen. A rare occurrence when I dare to cook.

However, the ghost doesn't materialize. She does leave a cryptic word in the flour—*truth.*

Not exactly the clarity I'm looking for about her identity.

Logan tells me the quiche is delicious and asks for second helpings. It feels nice to receive such a compliment. I only wish I could take credit. The whole time I'm preparing the dish, I feel the presence of the recipe owner guiding my hand.

The Honey Bar wraps around me like a warm peach cobbler when I push through the door a few hours later. The cute bee bells jingle overhead to announce my arrival. Lord have mercy, the smell of Brax's coffee can wake the dead, which is precisely what I'm trying to do, in a manner of speaking.

"Well, if it isn't Ava Fantome gracing us with her presence!" Marlene Jenkins calls from her usual corner table, lifting her mug in greeting.

I nod and smile, scanning the diner for the man in charge. The morning crowd is thick as Mississippi mud today, nearly every table filled with Thornhollow's finest, gossiping over steaming mugs and flaky pastries.

Brax is behind the counter, sleeves rolled up to his elbows, a five o'clock shadow framing his dark jawline as he juggles several orders at once. His movements remind me of a conductor leading an orchestra. He's precise yet somehow completely at home. He loves taking care of folks, just like his mama.

He glances up as I approach, his warm, brown eyes crinkling at the corners. "You look like you've been chasing ghosts all night."

I slide onto an empty stool, resting my elbows on the worn wood. "Any chance you've got a cup of that pecan brew left? I need something stronger than regular coffee, but it's too early for bourbon."

He grins, already reaching for my favorite mug—the one with "Bless Your Heart" written in loopy script. "Coming right up. You do look like you've seen a ghost, though. Any luck with our cook?"

"That's the problem," I sigh, drumming my fingers on the countertop. "She's MIA. I tried my usual tricks, but they didn't work. Although I did find my salt shaker knocked over this morning, and an invisible hand spelled 'truth' in the flour while I rolled out the breakfast quiche crust."

"You made quiche?"

I raise my chin. "Yes, and it was good, too."

He gives me an *I'm impressed* look. He slides the steaming mug toward me. "Truth, huh? Hmm. Guess that's what we all want at this point. To know the truth. Your guardian angel didn't drop by?"

I hadn't seen hide nor hair of Persephone since she revealed the skeleton to me. I wrap my hands around the warm ceramic. "Not a peep from her or the ghost cook. Not even a cold spot in the room. I spent a chunk of the night sitting in that dusty attic, talking to thin air, clutching those recipe cards like they were winning lottery tickets. I was so sure they'd help me connect with her. Especially when I cooked that quiche."

Brax wipes down the counter. "You know who might be able to help? Kit. That woman's got a direct line to the other side that makes Mama's prayer chain look like amateur hour."

"Already called her. Sage, too." The coffee is perfect—strong enough to put hair on a peach but sweet enough to make me forget I've been up all night. "Kit's supposed to meet me here this morning. I brought the recipe cards to show her. Maybe if she touches them, she'll get a hit. A name, a vision, a scent...anything would be helpful."

"You know, our legendary Birdie Birmingham disappeared back in the day. The most famous cook around. Could it be her?"

I sip more coffee, turning the idea over in my head. "I thought she ran off with a gangster or something and ended up in New Orleans."

Brax shrugs. "My granddaddy used to talk about her secret supper clubs. Said her blessing pie could fix broken hearts and her ghost stories would make your hair stand up straighter than a choir boy on Easter Sunday."

"Ghost stories, like the ones on the back of the recipes?"

"I suppose. I don't know if she ever wrote them down. Her recipes, either. Mama searched and searched for them for years, but never found any, not even at the historical society or library archives."

There goes that idea if it is Birdie.

"Why, she even reached out to Birdie's sister, but she was suffering from early-onset dementia." He clucks. "She couldn't remember anything about any recipes. From the stories about Birdie, she was one of those cooks who stored them all up here." He taps his temple.

"Hmm. It does kind of sound like her, though, doesn't it?"

"Can you imagine if it is? On this weekend of all weekends, when we're raising money for the charity?" He tosses the dishcloth aside and waves at a new round of customers announced by the jingling bell. He taps my mug with his fingertip. "I gotta go wait on some folks. Don't leave without saying goodbye, y'hear?"

Kit texts me to say she's running late. A second text comes from Sage. She'll be over to the house around ten. By the time Brax returns, I've finished my coffee and fended off two contestants in the cookoff who offered to buy me breakfast.

The attention isn't lost on him. He gives me a knowing grin as he hands off an order to his cook. "How does it feel to be the most popular gal in Thornhollow? I hear that new judge is gonna be real hard to win over."

I roll my eyes, though I can't help the small smile that tugs at my lips. "It's only been twelve hours, and I swear half the town has suddenly discovered they're my long-lost best friend."

"Your mama does have a way of making announcements. Heard she used the town emergency alert system."

"She *absolutely* did not—" I stop. Actually, that sounds like her. "Dixie Fantome has never met a microphone she didn't like and found multiple uses for."

Sadie Coltrain enters, clutching what appears to be a container. Her blue-tinted hair is piled impossibly high today, defying both gravity and good taste. She must have used an entire can of AquaNet this morning.

"If it isn't our esteemed judge!" Sadie's voice carries across the entirediner. "Avalon, honey, I was in the neighborhood and thought you might appreciate a little breakfast treat—no one can resist my peach cobbler."

I paste on my best professional smile. "How thoughtful."

"Now, you might notice I've added a splash of bourbon to the peaches," she stage-whispers, loud enough for half the patrons to hear. "And the crust? Secret family recipe. Been passed down since my great-great-grandmother served it to General Sherman himself. *Made him weep*, it did."

That's impressive, if it's true. "I'm sure it did, but I'm

afraid I can't accept your gracious offering if you're entering this in the cookoff. The other contestants might see it as bribery."

Before she can argue, Hank Pritchard sidles up, tipping his ever-present fishing hat. He stretches out his suspenders and lets them snap back. "Morning, Ava. Heard you're the new judge. That's real nice." He shifts from foot to foot. "Say, you remember those hushpuppies I brought to last fall's church social? The ones with the jalapeño and corn?"

"Vaguely." Logan compared them to deep-fried golf balls. Hence, I didn't touch them.

"Well, I've perfected the recipe." He pats his chest proudly. "Added a secret ingredient."

"Is it edible?" Brax mutters under his breath.

I pointedly pretend I didn't hear that. "Let me guess, you're entering them in the cookoff?"

"I sure am."

My cheeks are starting to ache from smiling. "Can't wait to try them there, then, Hank."

"I'll drop off a sample tomorrow," he promises, as if offering me the moon. "A little pre-cookoff gift."

Great. I'll alert Dr. Abernathy to have the stomach pump ready.

Louella Mae Thompson floats over in a cloud of floral perfume so strong it could wake a ghost. "Avalon, sugar!" She air-kisses my cheeks. "You look absolutely radiant today! Must be all that newlywed energy. That Logan Cross is a catch! Bet he keeps you busy." She gives me a devious wink.

"Thanks, Louella Mae," I say, wondering if she's been hitting the sherry early.

"Now, I don't want to influence you," she says, immediately preparing to do exactly that, "but my chicken and dumplings did win the blue ribbon at the county fair three years running. And this year, I've added a little something special."

"Let me guess," I say. "A secret ingredient?"

She gasps, seeming genuinely surprised. "How did you know?"

I catch Brax's eye as he turns away to hide his smirk. "Just a hunch."

"Well, it's a ghostly kind of pepper!" Louella Mae is nearly vibrating with excitement. "For a Southern Spirits theme! Get it? I thought you in particular would appreciate it."

She knows about my ghost-whispering. "Very clever," I tell her while I wish I could sink into the floor.

As Louella Mae rambles on about spice levels and dumpling consistency, I notice more townsfolk eyeing me from their tables, some holding recipe cards, while others take photos of me enjoying my coffee, as if documenting a celebrity sighting. If Persephone were here, she'd be having a field day with this parade of culinary bribery attempts.

"You know," I whisper to Brax once Louella Mae finally leaves. "I'm starting to understand why Birdie Birmingham might have disappeared. Maybe she was trying to escape being a food judge."

"Don't you go vanishing on us now." He chuckles as he refills my mug. "Though you might want to invest in some antacids."

I glance at the door, hoping Kit will arrive soon. Mrs. Hargrove waves enthusiastically to get my attention, a suspicious-looking mason jar of what might be pickled something-

or-other clutched in her hand. I turned back to stare at the counter.

Brax disappears into the back and returns with a golden-brown cornbread casserole, setting it to cool next to my coffee mug. "Care to try my jalapeño-honey cornbread? Just pulled it from the oven."

The casserole looks picture-perfect, steam still rising in delicate wisps. The aroma of sweet corn and butter mingles with the subtle kick of peppers, making my stomach growl traitorously.

"As tempting as that looks—and smells—I'm going to have to decline. That's what you're entering in the contest, right? Wouldn't want the good folks of Thornhollow crying favoritism."

Brax places a hand on his chest in mock offense. "Avalon Fantome-Cross, I would never dream of trying to influence a judge. This is merely breakfast hospitality."

"Uh-huh. And I'm sure that's exactly what you told Mrs. Wilkinson when she entered last year's pie contest that you judged."

"That was different," he protests, laughing. "Her bourbon pecan pie actually contained enough bourbon to get the Baptist choir tipsy."

"And your cornbread contains enough temptation to compromise my judicial integrity."

We're still laughing when the door swings open with such dramatic flair that the bell above the entrance gives an almost startled jingle. A tall, lean woman, dressed in a smart lilac suit, strides in, her heels clicking on the hardwood floor.

She pauses a few feet in, lowering her sunglasses and allowing everyone a moment to take in her carefully curated appearance—dark hair blown out to perfection, crimson lipstick precisely applied, and a cashmere scarf draped artfully over her shoulders despite the seventy-degree day. She's gripping her phone like it's an extension of her hand, no doubt ready for any impromptu photo opportunity.

Brax nearly drops his towel. He leans over the counter, lowering his voice. "Do you know who that is? That's Donna Dean."

"Who?"

He gives me a surprised face as if I just asked who Dolly Parton is. "Donna's Delicious Discoveries? The food blog?"

The woman scans the room until her gaze lands on me, her smile widening to reveal teeth so white they could signal passing ships. She makes her way over, stopping briefly to accept nods of recognition from patrons. Outside the diner, I notice a man watching through the window. Seems even passersby are enthralled with Donna's bigger-than-life presence.

"Avalon, right?" she says. "Just the judge I was hoping to see!"

"I am?" I force a smile, giving my achy cheeks another round of exercise.

She presents her hand, a giant emerald flashing under the lights. "Well, of course, silly."

I accept her handshake. "That's so...lovely. Have you come for breakfast?"

"Oh, I suppose your mama hasn't had a chance to tell you yet." She removes her designer sunglasses, and I note she's exceptionally pale. "I'll be joining you on the judging panel for the Southern Spirits Cookoff! Isn't that just divine?

The mayor thought my expertise as the South's premier food critic would lend credibility to the proceedings."

At my speechless reaction, she leans in to add in a whisper, "And she knew you might need help since you've never judged before. I'm your new mentor."

She straightens and gives me a wink.

"How nice of her," I say. "Always looking out for me."

And as Donna rattles on about her many accomplishments in the culinary world and how she's going to teach me all of them, all I can think is, *Mama, you owe me big time for this.*

Chapter Five

Donna's eyes drift to the casserole, and she inhales dramatically. "My goodness, what is that heavenly aroma?" She leans forward, hovering over Brax's creation. "It smells absolutely divine!"

Brax looks star-struck. I clear my throat and gesture toward him. "That's The Honey Bar's famous cornbread casserole made by the owner, Brax LaFleur."

Grabbing her phone, she takes a picture of it, then glances at Brax, batting her eyelashes. "You simply must tell me what's in it." Another dramatic inhale as if it were designer perfume. "My readers will go absolutely wild for a new recipe from a cute little diner like this."

Brax preens under her attention. His face lights up with a pleased grin, and he smooths down his apron. "You've got yourself quite the discerning palate. My recipe includes jalapeño and honey, along with my great-grandmama's secret ingredient."

"Oh?" Donna's perfectly plucked eyebrows arch

upward. She places a manicured hand on Brax's forearm, letting it linger. "And what might that be?"

"If I told you, it wouldn't be a secret now, would it?" Brax winks, reaching for a small plate. "Although, I reckon a small taste test wouldn't hurt. For professional purposes, of course."

"Of course," Donna purrs, watching intently as he cuts a generous square.

But I notice her rubbing her stomach. Not in the way of anticipating good food, but as if it's churning or cramping.

I catch Brax's eye and raise a brow, giving him my *you have always been a sucker for flattery* frown. He has the decency to look abashed, but he still slides the plate toward Donna.

"Oh my stars," Donna moans after her first bite. It's barely a forkful. "This is transcendent. The texture, the balance of sweet and heat." She shoots a quick peek over her shoulder, making sure everyone is watching. They are. A few more folks are peering through the windows. She closes her eyes in apparent ecstasy. "You've outdone yourself. Please tell me you're entering this in the contest."

So much for remaining impartial.

The door opens, causing a momentary diversion of attention from Donna's theatrical tasting. Kit stumbles in, looking like she's been through a small tornado. Her usually neat auburn hair sticks out in several directions, and dark circles shadow her eyes. She's wearing mismatched socks and what appears to be a pajama top.

"Coffee," she states, making a beeline for the counter. "Need coffee. Immediately."

"Kit Lyons without her morning coffee is like a live-action zombie movie," I muse, sliding off my stool to intercept her.

"Less talking, more caffeinating." She accepts the mug that Brax quickly sets out for her and downs half of its contents in one go, seemingly unfazed by the temperature.

"Rough night?" I ask as we move to a nearby table.

She slumps into the booth across from me. "Did I mention feeling a presence around my house last week?"

"A ghostly one?" I lower my voice, conscious of all the listening ears not far away. "No."

"A feline one," she corrects, taking another swig. "Turns out, a stray cat has decided I'm her new human. Last night, she showed up at three in the morning, yowling like a banshee under my bedroom window."

"And you let her in?" I already know the answer. Kit's no-nonsense exterior hides a marshmallow heart.

"What was I supposed to do? It started raining! So now I have a cat. I've named her Caboodle." She smiles, erasing the exhaustion lingering around her eyes. "Kit and Caboodle. Get it?"

I groan. "That's terrible."

Meanwhile, Donna hops off the stool and goes around the counter to take a selfie with Brax. Everyone's attention goes to them, except for one of the outside gawkers who scowls, shoulders his way through the gathered crowd, and disappears.

Kit raises her cup in a salute. "It's brilliant and you know it. Anyway, Caboodle decided that five a.m. was the perfect time to practice parkour across my furniture. My curtains are in shreds, my houseplants have been systematically destroyed, and somehow she's figured out how to turn on the bathroom faucet."

I laugh. "Sounds like quite the character."

"She's a menace," she says, but her voice is filled with affection. "A tiny, purring menace with murder mittens and no respect for personal boundaries." She rubs her eyes. "I swear she stares at things that aren't there. I wonder if she's seeing spirits."

Donna returns to her stool, continuing to chat up Brax. While Kit gulps her coffee, I lower my voice. "Speaking of spirits, I need your help with something strange." I reach into my bag and pull out the tin wrapped in a cotton scarf. "I had a visitor of my own last night."

Kit's gaze goes to the tin. "A ghost?"

"Persephone and Tabitha led me to an old trunk in the attic." I carefully unwrap the scarf to reveal the recipe tin and use the edge of the material to lift the lid, revealing the cards inside. "We found something up there. Well, two somethings, actually. A skeleton—"

Kit chokes on her coffee. "A what now?"

"A skeleton. Human." I add this last bit unnecessarily, as if there were some confusion about what kind of skeleton might be hidden in a Georgia attic.

"Sweet heavens!" Kit's eyes are now fully alert, caffeine boost apparently unnecessary in the face of my macabre hidden treasure.

"Detective Jones took the remains for identification, but here's where it gets interesting." I tap the recipe cards. "These were under the skeleton's hand. A spirit was there, a woman, and she tried to tell me something, but then vanished. I haven't been able to connect with her again, but I suspect there's foul play involved, and it involves these cards."

"Well, yeah, that seems obvious."

"These recipes are strange, though, and have ghost stories written on the backs. They also have a hand-drawn bird in the corner, maybe a signature or insignia? Brax suggested they might have belonged to Birdie Birmingham." Turning the theory over in my mind, I find it intriguing. "I think he might be right."

Kit's expression shifts from shocked to intrigued. "*The* Birdie Birmingham? The blessing pie lady? I didn't know a thing about her until I started seeing all this stuff about the cookoff and her charity." She snaps her fingers. "Wait, didn't she run off with some guy back in the day?"

"There's some disagreement about what happened to her, but she definitely disappeared in the sixties." Being both a psychic and a private detective makes Kit uniquely qualified for this particular mystery. "I've tried everything to connect with the ghost." Frustration seeps into my voice. "Nothing is working. But these cards are important. I was hoping you could touch them and get a hit off of them. Tell me if I'm on the right track about Birdie."

Kit sets down the mug and wipes her hands on a napkin, all business now. She reaches for the tin. "May I?"

"Please." I slide it across the table. "I brought these." I pull out a pair of latex gloves. "Logan believes the tin and cards could be evidence, so we can't get fingerprints on them. Can you still get a hit if you wear gloves?"

"Maybe," she says, pulling them on. "Shouldn't you give these to Detective Jones if you think they have something to do with the skeleton's death?"

"I plan to. I want to see if I can connect with her spirit first. She could be the key to solving this and saving everyone a lot of time and energy. Even the detective."

"Makes sense."

The bustling diner fades into the background as Kit takes the recipe cards, turning them over in her slender fingers. Her eyes close briefly. Her breathing slows, taking on the rhythm of a tide pulling something unseen toward her. This is Kit in her element, tapping into something beyond what most of us can perceive.

I hold my breath, watching her face for any sign, any hint that she's connecting with Birdie's spirit—or whoever the skeleton is. The cheerful chatter of The Honey Bar continues around us, but at our table, time seems to stand still.

A crease forms between her brows. Her fingers trace the faded printing on one card—a recipe for blackberry cobbler with peculiar notes in the margin about moonlight and hexes. The temperature around our table seems to drop by several degrees, and I resist the urge to rub my arms.

"There's something here," Kit murmurs, her voice distant. "Something protective. These recipes weren't just about food."

My pulse quickens. "What do you mean?"

"Your ghost wasn't only cooking. I think she was *casting*." Kit's eyes are still closed. "This is Sage's area of expertise, but I'd bet money that these are more than recipes—they're spells. Protection spells, blessing spells, hexes even, all disguised as southern comfort food."

She opens her eyes, which seem darker now, the pupils bigger. "Whoever killed her—and yes, Ava, someone definitely killed her—they were after these. But they couldn't use them."

My worst fear is confirmed. "Why not?"

"I'm not sure, but it feels like there's a block of some kind around them. Something that feels like scandals and betrayal." She rubs her temple. "My head is pounding from it. It's keeping me out."

A chill trails down my spine that has nothing to do with The Honey Bar's overzealous air conditioning. "So her killer didn't get what they wanted? But if she had this tin when she died, why didn't they take it?"

"Sorry, I can't tell you that. It's her unfinished business, and I suspect it goes much deeper than these recipes. It feels like it's about her life's work remaining incomplete."

Her expression shifts abruptly, her gaze darting over my shoulder toward the counter. "Ava," she whispers, "something's wrong."

I turn to follow her line of sight. Donna Dean is perched on her barstool, one hand gripping the counter's edge while the other clutches at her belly. The confident food blogger who'd been flirting with Brax minutes ago now sways precariously, her already pale complexion draining to the color of uncooked biscuit dough.

"She looks sick," I say, but Kit's already standing, the recipes forgotten.

Donna's eyes widen, panic flickering across her features. She tries to speak, but only manages a choked gasp. The half-eaten piece of Brax's cornbread casserole sits abandoned before her.

"Brax!" I call out. He's in the kitchen, and he comes

running out the swinging door, moving around the counter with surprising speed for such a big man.

Donna's eyes roll back. She slides sideways, crumpling to the floor with a sickening thud that seems to echo through the suddenly silent diner.

"Oh my Lord," someone gasps.

I rush toward her, Kit on my heels.

"Don't move her," Kit commands as Brax starts to reach for her. Kit gently tilts Donna's head to check her airway. It appears clear. "Ava, call nine-one-one."

"What happened?" My voice sounds strangely distant as I grab my purse and fumble for my phone.

The diner patrons form a semicircle around us, their faces lit with horror, curiosity, and the anticipation of gossip to come. Brax hovers, wiping his hands on his dish towel and waving them back. "Is she breathing?"

My call connects, and I give the operator the details, even as Kit begins CPR. I guess the answer to that question is *no*. "We need an ambulance at The Honey Bar on Main Street. A woman has collapsed."

The operator asks for my name and tells me to stay on the line. I move my fingers to Donna's neck, searching for the carotid pulse, and that's when I notice a thin line of white foam at the corner of her mouth.

"Sweet mercy," I whisper. I grab Donna's designer bag and dump out its contents.

"What are you doing?" someone asks.

"Looking for a medical card or EpiPen," I reply.

"Food allergy?" Brax asks.

I can't find either. "Possibly, but there's nothing here to indicate she has one."

The murmuring around us intensifies. "Is she...?" asks Mrs. Hempshaw.

"Did she just keel over from Brax's cooking?" questions Old Man Jenkins, tactful as ever.

"Donna? Donna, can you hear me?" Brax gently pats her cheek as Kit continues CPR. He looks at me with desperate eyes. "She was fine, laughing and flirting and..." He trails off, glancing at the half-eaten piece of cornbread casserole still sitting on the counter.

"Don't touch anything, Brax," I tell him quietly. "Especially not that casserole."

Brax flinches as if I've slapped him. "You think *my casserole* did something to her?"

I can no longer feel any pulse. Donna's glazed, lifeless eyes stare up at the ceiling. My heart sinks as I realize what this could mean.

The distant wail of sirens cuts through the space.

Help is coming.

Too bad it's too late.

Chapter Six

The door of The Honey Bar slams open with such force that the welcome bell shrieks in protest. Two paramedics rush in with a stretcher and medical equipment, their faces calm yet hurried. Reverend Stout is one of them. He quickly approaches with a plastic medic's box and waves me aside. "What happened?"

Gray-haired and wrinkled, he wears the standard white shirt and navy pants of our first responder. A name tag is pinned above the pocket of his shirt, where a protector filled with pens and a tiny flashlight is secured inside. Most days, he can be found at the church, rescuing souls. Today, he's an EMT, working on physical bodies rather than spiritual ones with his coworker, Wesley.

Donna lies motionless, her perfectly coiffed blonde hair splayed across the hardwood in a tragic halo. My throat feels tight as I speak. "She just collapsed."

The good reverend and Wesley move with choreographed efficiency, kneeling beside Donna's still form.

Wesley checks Donna's neck for a pulse and asks questions, noting the foam around her mouth. Brax answers, explaining when Donna arrived, what happened, and how Kit already attempted CPR.

Wesley attaches leads to Donna's chest and fires up the defibrillation machine.

The restaurant is cemetery-quiet. The usual din of clinking cutlery and brewing coffee is gone, replaced by their clipped instructions to each other and the sound of the machine. When Wesley calls, "Clear," we all step back, as if the defibrillator might zap us.

I hold my breath, as if breathing might somehow jinx whatever slim chance Donna has. Her body jerks, but the monitor is silent. Wesley recharges it, and there's another round.

And another.

After what seems like both an eternity and no time at all, Stout motions for Wesley to stop. The young man sits back on his heels and checks his watch. "Time of death, nine forty-seven AM."

A collective gasp ripples through the onlookers, followed by a heavy silence. The words hang in the air like summer humidity—thick, oppressive, impossible to ignore. Outside, the gathered crowd seems to understand what's transpired, and folks shake their heads, cover their mouths, and one woman tears up.

"Are you sure?" Kit asks. "Shouldn't you try something else?"

Reverend Stout shakes his head, compassion softening his demeanor. "I'm sorry. She's gone." He gently squeezes her arm. "You did what you could."

The silence shatters as Detective Jones strides in, boots clunking and presence looming. Those bushy eyebrows of his are drawn together, accentuating his perpetual scowl. He's never been what you'd call a ray of sunshine, but there's something reassuring about his no-nonsense approach right now. He doesn't waste time on pleasantries or beating around the bush.

"Detective," Reverend Stout acknowledges. "Female victim, approximately forty years old. No obvious trauma."

Jones nods curtly. "Cause of death?"

"Can't confirm without the ME." The reverend lowers his voice, though in the silent restaurant, we all hear him anyway. "The blue tinge to her lips, the sudden onset, and the foam at her mouth are all suggestive of acute poisoning."

When Mrs. Hempshaw tries to escape out the door, Jones raises his voice. "Everyone, stay where you are. This is now an active investigation scene."

My knees go weak. *Poisoning.* Just as I suspected.

In The Honey Bar, my friend's restaurant. "No," I blurt out before I can stop myself. I've seen it with my own eyes, but... "That's impossible."

Jones turns those penetrating eyes my way, and I swear the temperature drops ten degrees. He's never appreciated my tendency to speak my mind, especially at crime scenes. "Ms. Fantome," he says flatly, using my maiden name because he knows it annoys me. It's his little way of putting me in my place. "I see you're involved. Again."

"I was just having coffee with Kit," I protest, trying to keep the defensive edge from my voice. It doesn't work.

Two officers join us, and he addresses them without acknowledging my reply. "Secure the scene. Nobody leaves.

Get a list of everyone who was in this establishment in the last hour."

The other officers don gloves and begin snapping pictures and video.

"Any food or drink consumed by the victim should be preserved for testing," Jones continues, his gaze landing on Donna's plate and then on Brax's cornbread casserole.

Brax braces his feet and puts his hands on his hips. "I didn't poison anyone."

"Did you serve her that?"—Jones points at the cornbread with his pen.

"Yes, but—"

"Did she eat or drink anything else?"

Brax's voice falters. "No, but—"

Jones studies the casserole and sniffs the air. "Did you serve any of this to anyone else?"

The smell of the honey-jalapeño cornbread suddenly seems sinister. Brax flicks a fearful gaze to me. "No, but—"

"I can't stay here all morning," one of the customers complains. I don't know him and suspect he may be a tourist. "I have things to do."

Jones turns to glare at him. "Tough. Everyone, remain calm and seated. This may take a while."

I catch Kit's eye, and we share a look of mutual dismay. This isn't just a tragedy—it's about to become a full-blown scandal in our little town. And poor Brax is right in the middle of it.

Jones strides to the kitchen, and we tag after him. The cook, Okie Simpson, looks to be in shock. Brax vacillates between looking faint and ready to tear into Jones for his unstated accusations.

"Just breathe," I whisper to my friend.

"Start at the beginning." Jones pulls out his notepad. "Walk me through the timeline of what happened. What did you observe about Ms. Dean before she collapsed?"

Brax's voice comes out calm, even though I know he's anything but. He gives Jones the blow-by-blow details. Jones writes it all down, his pen scratching across the paper. He turns to Okie and fires a series of questions at him, but Okie sheds no light on the cooking of the casserole. "Brax handled it." His eyes are sheepish as he glances at his boss. "It's his special recipe. He won't share it, even with me."

"Interesting," Jones says in a tone that suggests he finds it *very* interesting indeed. "This entire kitchen is now a crime scene. No one touches anything."

Brax jams a hand through his hair. Okie flinches. At the counter, a deputy swoops in with an evidence bag, carefully scooping up the casserole dish as if it were radioactive waste, while another marches into the kitchen with yellow crime scene tape.

"Detective," I start, trying to sound reasonable, "surely you don't think—"

Jones cuts me off. "I think the medical examiner will confirm poisoning, and I think your friend here needs to come down to the station to answer questions."

Brax makes a small, exasperated sound.

"You can't seriously be treating this as murder already," Kit protests. "This could be an allergic reaction, or—"

"Or it could be oleander mixed into cornbread," Jones replies dryly. "Let the professionals handle this, Ms. Lyons."

I shake my head. "Well, that escalated quickly." A

memory surfaces. "She was acting sick before she fell off the stool, rubbing her stomach."

He ignores me and turns to Brax, whose dark skin has gone ash gray. "Mr. LaFleur, I'm going to need you to come with me. We have questions about the preparation of the food Ms. Dean consumed and your relationship with her."

"Relationship?" Brax looks stricken. "I've never even met her until this morning. What motive would I have to kill her?"

"Save it for the station," Jones says, not unkindly but firmly. "Deputy Ramirez will escort you."

As Ramirez sets down the crime scene tape with a sympathetic-just-doing-my-job expression that cops perfect in their first year, I feel a surge of protective anger.

"I'm calling Logan," I tell Brax, squeezing his arm. "Don't say anything until he gets there."

Jones gives me a look that could curdle sweet tea. "Involving your husband already? Do you know something you're not telling me?"

Must he always jump to conclusions? "Brax is innocent, but I'm ensuring he has proper legal representation during questioning about a death you've already decided is murder."

For a moment, Jones and I stare each other down like two cats on a fence. Finally, he shrugs. "Call whoever you want." He nods to Ramirez. "Let's go."

As they lead Brax away, his cornbread casserole now sealed in the evidence bag, I turn to Kit with the pit of something hard and heavy in my chest. "This is crazy, Brax never hurt anyone."

Kit nods, her eyes tracking the departing police. "Jones has always been quick to judgment."

"Well, he's wrong." I grab my phone to call Logan. "And we're going to prove it."

Three rings later, my husband's warm, comforting voice fills my ear. "Hey, there. I was just about to—"

"I need your lawyer brain." My voice cracks. I'm short of breath. "Donna Dean, the food blogger, collapsed at The Honey Bar a few minutes ago. Jones believes she was poisoned. Brax is being taken to the station under suspicion of having done it with his cornbread casserole."

There's a moment of silence, and I hear the gears turning in his head, shifting from whatever he was working on to this. "I'm on my way. You were there when it happened?"

"I'm still here. I need to notify Queenie and Rhys."

His tone is all business, but there's that underlying steadiness that's like a security blanket for my fraying nerves. "Don't do anything I wouldn't do, okay? Let Jones handle the investigation, and let me handle Brax's defense."

I bite my lip. Logan, of course, would leave the investigation in the hands of the police. He would absolutely not go off on his own to hunt down a suspect. "Hurry," is all I say, because I'm about to do exactly that.

His sigh holds equal parts exasperation and affection. "This food blogger...any chance her ghost has reached out to you?"

I glance around, but she's not here. At least, not that I can tell. "Nope. Not sure she could tell us anything even if she was hanging around. She wouldn't know who poisoned her."

We disconnect, and I feel equal amounts of relief and worry. "Logan's on his way," I tell Kit. "He'll meet Brax at the station and get this cleared up."

At least, I hope so.

Chapter Seven

One of the deputies takes everyone's statements, and the body is sealed in a black bag and removed. The diner feels emptier, colder. I can't stop looking at the outline on the floor left by the officers.

The place needs to be shut down. As Kit and I escort Okie home and verify all the ovens are off, Queenie LaFleur storms in. Her signature black beehive wobbles dangerously as she comes to a complete stop and assesses the scene, hands on hips.

"What in tarnation is going on?" Her voice carries that special blend of Southern command that can make grown men come to attention. Her eyes dart from me to Kit to the remaining officer cataloging evidence. "Where is my son?"

I've known her my whole life, but she still intimidates me sometimes. At sixty-two, she has the energy of someone half her age and the will of someone twice as stubborn. No wonder she and Mama are best friends.

Once again, I relate the story of Donna showing up,

eating the casserole, and ending up dead. Queenie's eyes grow rounder and rounder. "They've taken Brax to the station for questioning. Detective Jones thinks Ms. Dean was poisoned by his casserole."

Queenie's voice rises an octave. "My Braxton wouldn't poison a possum if it was eating his prize tomatoes. He catches spiders in cups and releases them outside, for heaven's sake!"

Kit rubs her arm, her jaw set with determination. "We're going to figure this out."

Queenie marches over to the remaining customers huddled in shocked clusters near one of the long tables. "I'm sorry, y'all, but we're closing early for obvious reasons." Her tone leaves no room for argument, though her hands are trembling slightly as she shoos people toward the door.

When the last customer reluctantly departs, she flips the sign and turns the deadbolt with a decisive click. The yellow crime scene tape left behind to mark off the area around where Donna fell glares at us under the overhead lights.

"This is a nightmare." She collapses onto a barstool. "Who would want to hurt that woman? She's practically a legend."

"Jones is looking for the obvious culprit," I say, pacing between tables. "Brax cooked the food, so he's it."

Queenie snorts. "Obvious to a fool, maybe. Brax has no motive!"

My mind spins. I stop pacing and face both women. "Then we need to find out who does. If it truly is murder, who would benefit from Donna's death?"

"Ava..." Kit says with that warning tone she uses when I'm about to dive headfirst into trouble.

I cross my arms against the fear and doubt lurking in my chest. "Brax is like my brother. I'm not letting him take the fall for something he didn't do."

Queenie straightens her spine, her eyes suddenly sharp. "Me, either, but what can we do?"

"Kit has her intuition and is a solid private detective. Queenie, you know everyone in this town, and I've picked up a thing or two about investigations from my dad."

Kit sighs, but I can see resignation in her eyes. "Jones isn't going to like us poking around."

"Jones can kiss my grits," I reply.

This earns a surprised laugh from Queenie. "I'm gonna embroider those exact five words on a tea towel."

I'd take one of those myself. "We need to figure out who might have held a grudge against Donna. No one could have known that Brax was cooking his casserole this morning and that Donna would end up here eating it. That's too much of a coincidence. But she might have been poisoned before she even arrived."

Queenie's eyes narrow thoughtfully. "Ms. Dean has—had—plenty of enemies."

"Like who?" Kit asks.

Queenie fiddles with her beehive. "I used to like her when she was focused on bringing folks good recipes. Then she started trashing small diners and drive-ins, giving them horrible reviews, and her popularity skyrocketed. I once wanted her to feature my place, but now see what a bullet I dodged. It's sad that so many folks thrive on that sort of thing. Once she had an audience, she began searching for restaurants with scandalous histories that she could spotlight for her own gain. One blog or video from her could make or break a restaurant's reputation. She's bankrupted more than twenty of them throughout the South in the past few years."

I straighten. "That's motive. We need to follow up on those."

Queenie hesitates. "You really think someone poisoned her out of revenge?"

"If she had done that to your restaurant or this one"—I gesture around at the diner—"wouldn't you want revenge?"

Her eyes harden. "You know I would."

Rhys appears at the door, his T-shirt wrinkled and half-untucked, his hair standing up like he's been running his hands through it repeatedly. His freckles are dark marks against his pale face.

Queenie unlocks the door for him and he hugs her before rushing over to me and Kit. "Is it true?" His eyes are wild as they dart around the now-empty bar and land on the body outline. "Eek!" He whirls away. "Someone said—they said Brax *poisoned* Donna Dean. Is she really...?" He can't seem to form the word "dead," and his Adam's apple bobs.

"Rhys," Kit says gently. "Why don't you sit down?"

He ignores her, zeroing in on me. "Ava, please. Just tell me what happened." His hands shake, and there's something in his expression beyond just shock—a raw panic over these terrible circumstances.

I lead him to the booth where Kit and I shared coffee. "Ms. Dean is dead, and Detective Jones thinks she was poisoned. She ate a portion of Brax's cornbread casserole right before it happened."

Rhys collapses into the booth. "How awful," he whispers.

I slide in next to him and put an arm around his shoulders. "Logan's on his way to help Brax, and Kit and I are going to find out what really happened."

Kit slides in on the other side. Her coffee cup and mine bookend the tin of recipes. "Nobody's going to railroad Brax for something he didn't do."

As Rhys glances between us, I see a flicker of something —relief? Fear?—cross his face.

The recipe tin wobbles, then levitates. We all recoil and Kit gasps. "Ava...?"

I can't see the spirit lifting it, but it's obvious someone is there. "Hello?" I say. "Donna? Is that you?"

I hear a disappointed *tsk*. The tin falls to the table.

Does that mean no?

I try again. "Ghost from my attic? This is your tin, right? Your recipes?"

The tin shoots straight up.

My heart hammers. "Are you Birdie Birmingham?"

The tin flies at the wall, crashes, and the recipes fall out, scattering over the table and falling into our laps.

Wish I knew if that meant yes or no. I don't.

One of the cards skitters across the table without being touched, coming to a stop in front of me.

Queenie stands a few feet away. "What does it say?" she asks, her voice shaking.

I stare at the recipe card, its edges worn soft with age. "Expose-a-Secret Shortbread," I read aloud, my throat suddenly dry.

Kit's eyes meet mine, wide with understanding. "She's trying to tell us something. About what happened to Donna. It's a secret, right?"

The lights flicker once, twice. I try not to flinch. "I think that's a yes."

"Well." Kit's voice is steady despite everything. "Looks like we have another investigator joining our team." She addresses the empty air. "Ms. Birmingham, if you're here to help us clear Brax's name, we sure would appreciate it."

Queenie glances around, looking skeptical and a little bit unnerved. "Birdie Birmingham? Her ghost is *here*?"

"I'll find out what happened to you, too," I tell her with a nod at Queenie. "I'll find justice for both of you."

A single electric bulb over the bar pops in response, showering tiny glass fragments onto the counter.

"I'll take that as your agreement." I return the recipe cards to the tin. "I may not be a detective, but I've got you and your recipes, and I'm not afraid to use them."

Chapter Eight

The May humidity clings to me as I step through my front door.

I haven't even kicked off my shoes or dropped my purse on my desk inside my office when the scents of magnolias and fresh-brewed tea greet me.

Arthur and Lancelot laze in the display window, barely opening their eyes when I pet each of them. Moxley says hello with a raspy woof and trots ahead of me as if escorting me to the kitchen.

My kitchen—normally my sanctuary of calm—is buzzing with energy that has nothing to do with my new ghostly visitor. Rosie waves at me from the table. She's in a cute, pale yellow linen pant suit with a floral blouse. "There she is! Sweet mercy, you look like you've seen a—" She catches herself. "Well, I suppose you might have seen a ghost, but this is different."

Sage sits across from her. She's twisted her long hair into an elaborate braid adorned with tiny sprigs of rosemary.

She's a natural-born witch and a good friend who's helped me deal with uncooperative spirits and cursed objects. Her crimson tunic is sleeveless, revealing a new phoenix tattoo, and she's wearing a skirt layered in three tiers of lavender cotton. Her slender fingers tap against my Aunt Willa's favorite china teacup. "We heard," she says. "About Donna Dean at The Honey Bar. The news is all over town."

I let Moxley out the back door so he can mosey around the yard before I drop into a chair next to her. I release a long exhale. "Well, that didn't take long."

"Honey, this is Thornhollow," Rosie reminds me, adjusting her sleeves. "News travels faster than kudzu on a south-facing wall, but we got the inside scoop from Logan before he tore out of here to go to the station."

Sage's eyes, green as spring leaves, are pensive. "The energy around sudden deaths is always so chaotic." She shivers, and I notice the protective crystals around her wrist catching the late morning light coming through the kitchen window. "Did her spirit speak to you before she crossed?"

"No, but the ghost from my attic did."

Rosie chokes. "The ghost from your attic?"

So she hasn't heard about *that* yet. I fill them in on the skeleton, the tin, and the recipes. They both blink and ask questions. "I don't know much about her yet, but all signs point to it being Birdie Birmingham. I just have to confirm it." I wave it away. "For now, that's the least of my worries. I have to clear Brax's name."

"It's just terrible." Sage toys with her bracelets. "He must be so upset."

"He is. So is Queenie."

"Donna was staying at the Nottingham," Rosie says.

"Baldwin and Kalina were beside themselves with excitement when she booked. They had this big live event planned for tonight—a live cooking demonstration, book signing, the works. I had tickets!" She shakes her head in disappointment. "Baldwin and Kalina are panicking something fierce."

Those two run a haunted hotel. Not much makes them panic. "Because they're worried about refunding folks' money?"

"Nah, not that. Think about it." Rosie sips some tea. "A famous food blogger dies right after arriving at their hotel? People are gonna wonder what she might have ate *there*."

I sit back and consider it. "That might be the key to clearing Brax's name, though."

Sage sighs. "Kalina scheduled a special tea party for Mother's Day at the shop. She called me in tears. Said they were hoping Donna's visit would put them on the culinary map. Now they're afraid it'll put them on the obituary page."

I bite my bottom lip and pull out my phone. I commiserate with their predicament, but I feel hope for Brax. "I need to talk to them and find out exactly when Donna arrived, who she spoke with, and what she ate and drank before heading to The Honey Bar."

Sage gets up to pour me a cup of tea. "Poor Brax. I feel so bad for him." She slides it toward me. It smells of chamomile and something earthy. "Valerian root. For your nerves," she says, gesturing for me to drink up.

I sip and try not to make a face. I add honey from the jar on the table, then dial Baldwin's cell number. "It's shaken him to his core, and honestly, it looks bad for him."

"Ava?" Kalina's voice is a screech. She must be fielding personal calls while her husband handles the business ones.

"It's absolute chaos here! Please tell me your husband will represent us if there's a lawsuit."

And there it is. The real fear: liability. I put her on speaker. "Of course he will. Now, tell me everything you know about Donna. When did she arrive? What did she eat or drink while she was there? Anything might help."

Her voice drops to a whisper. "Detective Jones is here. He's questioning everyone like we're on one of those crime shows. We've already supplied him with all the details. Donna had a coffee and a breakfast sandwich with her when she arrived. I have no idea where she got them."

I can picture Detective Jones—his dark, imposing figure, hulking around and making accusations like he did with Brax. I want to reach through the phone and squeeze her hand in support. "Anything else you noticed about her? Anything at all?"

"Nothing important. She said she wanted to explore the town before her event tonight. That's it! I swear!"

I sigh. "And she seemed fine? Nothing unusual? She didn't seem overly pale to you? No obvious stomach issues?"

"She was delightful, if a bit wan. I worried she was getting sick, but she claimed she was fine. She took photos of the sandwich for her social media and said our formal garden was 'utterly charming'. We were planning to quote her everywhere!"

I'm not the only one who noticed she looked sick. "Be sure you tell Jones about her appearing sick, and if you think of anything else, call me immediately, okay?"

"I will, but... Oh no, Jones is coming. I have to go!" The line goes dead.

I sip more tea, wishing it were iced. "A breakfast sandwich and coffee. Apparently, Donna brought both to the hotel when she checked in this morning. That's our best lead at this point."

Rosie refills her cup. "I'm sure Jones is already looking into Donna's breakfast. Best to steer clear until the autopsy results come back. I assume they're doing one, right?"

"I assume. Doc is probably beside himself. He's got a skeleton and a fresh body to examine."

Sage closes her eyes for a moment as if she's sending him some positive energy. "Jones needs a serious aura cleansing." She opens her eyes and wiggles her fingers. "His energy is porcupine prickly."

"It's not his aura, it's his personality," I reply with a half-smile, staring into my teacup, watching the leaves swirl in patterns. Sage could probably interpret my future with them.

She taps a finger on the table. "Enough about Donna Dean for a minute. Tell us more about this skeleton."

"Just another day at Enchanted Events," Rosie teases.

I'm almost grateful to the topic change. "You act like finding human remains is an everyday occurrence for me."

Both of them know exactly how often the dead decide to make my life complicated and Sage laughs softly. "With you, I'm surprised it doesn't happen weekly."

It kind of does. "All I know is that the ghost *is* trying to communicate, and she's sent me more than one message. Oh." I snap my fingers. "I have her recipe cards." I leave the table to grab them from my purse and return, setting the tin on the table. "This was hers, and I think they belonged to Birdie Birmingham."

"Birdie?" Rosie repeats with surprise. "*Our* Birdie Birmingham?"

I mentally run through what I've learned about her so far. "I'm pretty certain. I don't know how she ended up inside that trunk with these recipes, but I need to find out. It may be the only way to bring her peace and help her move on. Kit says there's a block around them, and that may be why the ghost isn't able to talk to me."

Sage stirs honey into her own tea, her teaspoon clinking against the china. "Some spirits are bound by rules we don't understand. The block may be on her and that's why she can't speak directly."

"Or maybe she doesn't remember everything," I suggest.

Rosie toys with her cup. "How do you know for sure it's her?"

"I don't. Not completely, but when I asked the spirit at the diner questions, it seemed to respond and confirm it was. She seems to want to help with Donna's death."

The front door opens and Kit races in, looking like she's swallowed a canary. Or rather, carrying one—because nestled in her arms is the tiniest ball of gray and white fluff I've ever seen. "Meet Caboodle," she announces proudly, her voice charged in that way people always have around babies and small animals.

"Oh my stars!" Rosie exclaims, murder and ghosts instantly forgotten as she rises from her chair to stroke the kitten.

Sage coos, her hands reaching out in invitation. "Where did you find this precious little creature?"

"She showed up at my door last night." Kit transfers the kitten to Sage and drops a handful of cat toys on the table. "Poor thing was soaking wet from the rain. I thought all the banging around outside was a possum or a spirit. Found this, instead."

Its eyes are barely open—bright blue slits in a face that seems ninety percent ears. As I reach over to stroke its head, there's a thump from the living room, followed by the rapid patter of paws. Tabby appears in the doorway, tail twitching. She approaches, whiskers forward, every movement deliberate.

She jumps up on the table and I hurriedly slide our cups out of the way. She sniffs once at the kitten, then bumps her head against Sage's arm as if to say, "Hand it over."

"Well, would you look at that." Rosie laughs as Sage carefully places Caboodle on the floor. Tabby immediately jumps down and begins grooming the kitten. Caboodle responds with a squeaky mew that melts even my death-preoccupied heart.

"I think we've been adopted," Kit says, watching as Tabby herds the kitten toward the living room, pausing occasionally to make sure the little one is following.

We all watch as they disappear, Caboodle's tiny tail held high in imitation of his new mentor.

For that moment, death and ghosts seem far away.

Chapter Nine

"The poor soul," Rosie murmurs, smoothing her already-smooth napkin. "Birdie, I mean. Imagine being stuck in that trunk for what, fifty-odd years?"

Back to death and dying. "Might have been nice if Persephone had led me to the trunk sooner."

"Maybe she didn't know," Kit says.

That *is* possible. Persephone knows a lot, but not everything, even if she acts like she does. "I wish I knew more about Birdie. What was she like? Who might've wanted her dead? What secrets was she keeping?"

Sage's eyes light up. "We should try a séance."

Kit gives me a smirk. Sage is *always* up for a séance. "I don't know. Ava's ghosts *never* cooperate when we do those."

Sage is already rummaging in her voluminous purse. She produces a small velvet pouch that clinks with what I know are her special crystals. "There are four of us. We can do it."

With me, Sage, Rosie, and Kit, we have enough to form a circle. However, I'm with Kit. "My experiences with these things usually go sideways, and I end up possessed, astral traveling, or dead."

Sage draws out the crystals. "I'll keep you grounded. Since you have a connection with her, we just need you to lend your voice. Like spiritual karaoke."

I snort. "Spiritual karaoke? Is that what they're teaching at witch school these days?"

Sage gives me a look that's half amusement, half exasperation. "Mock if you must, but séances have connected the living with the dead for centuries. With the right preparation and respect, we might be able to hear what Birdie's been trying to tell you. Grab a candle, one of those recipe cards, and let's get started."

I consider it, watching as she begins to arrange the crystals in a pattern.

"I'm not sure about this." Rosie rubs the cross pendant at her throat. She flicks her worried gaze between us. "Y'all aren't worried about... I don't know, opening doors that should stay closed? What if we call in something with more teeth than manners?"

It's a fair question. I want justice for a woman whose bones were hidden away in a trunk for half a century. For a celebrated cook who vanished without a trace, leaving behind nothing but recipes and rumors. But when you invite spirit in, you never know what might piggyback on it.

Through the doorway, I catch a glimpse of Tabby and Caboodle curled together on the sofa, the kitten tucked safely against my cat's side. "Actually," I say, setting my teacup aside, "before we go summoning spirits, why don't we try something a little more straightforward?"

Sage's face falls slightly. "You don't want to do the séance?"

"I'm not saying no to it," I clarify, "I'm saying let's do some digging first. If we're going to communicate with Birdie's ghost, shouldn't we know who we're talking to?"

Rosie nods, visibly relieved. "That makes sense. Hard to ask the right questions if you don't know much about the person."

"Exactly." I tap my fingers against the worn top of my kitchen table. How many times did I sit here with my aunt and uncle when I was a kid? Now it's with my husband and friends. "We need background. Context. Birdie Birmingham was a real person before she became a ghost in my attic. She had a life, friends, family, a whole history."

"Good old-fashioned research," Kit says. "Sometimes the simplest approach is best. Going to call the town gossips? The historical society?"

"Already on it with both, but right now, let's try the internet."

I head to my office, stepping carefully over a toy mouse that my cats have abandoned in the hallway. When I return, Rosie has cleared a space among the teacups and Caboodle's scattered toys.

I set my laptop down. "What do we know about her so far?" This morning, I searched for recipes and ghost stories before I knew who might have created them. Now, I have a solid lead and type the info into the search engine. "Birdie Birmingham, Southern cook, disappeared around 1966 from Thornhollow."

The results begin to populate the screen. I lean forward, scanning the headlines. "Here we go. *Birdie Birmingham:*

The Vanished Voice of Southern Cooking. It's an article from the Georgia Historical Society from September of 1966."

The honey pot begins trembling. All eyes go to it, including mine. "Okay..." I say. "Birdie? Is that you?"

It spins in a perfect circle. The others gape with wide eyes.

"I want to learn more about you, so I'm doing what's called an internet search." I tap the link to the article. "This is a computer and it can access information from all over the world at lightning speed."

The article loads, revealing a black-and-white photograph of a woman with soft waves in her hair and an apron tied around her waist. Her warm eyes seem to look right through the camera, as if she's sharing a secret with the photographer. "That's her," I breathe, showing the others the screen. "That's Birdie."

Sage and Kit both shift to look over my shoulder. Sage leans so close, her braid brushes my shoulder. "She looks kind. Like someone who'd slip you an extra cookie when your mama wasn't looking."

The honey pot bounces and settles. "Looks like you're right," Kit says.

"Listen to this." I scan the paragraphs, reading aloud. *"Birdie Birmingham, celebrated for her culinary expertise and storytelling abilities, hosted what became known as 'Birdie's Secret Suppers' throughout the early 1960s. These exclusive gatherings were invitation-only affairs where guests enjoyed her legendary cooking while she regaled them with ghost stories and Southern folklore."*

"Secret suppers," Rosie says in a swoony voice. "How deliciously scandalous."

I scroll to the next paragraph and suck in a breath. "Get this! Her most frequent venue? It was none other than the Nottingham Hotel!"

Kit's eyebrows shoot up. "No way. That's quite a coincidence."

I continue reading. *"Birmingham was known for her 'blessing pie,' said to bring good fortune to anyone who consumed it. She claimed she never wrote down her recipes for fear someone would steal them, but she was reportedly working on a cookbook titled 'Cooking with Ghosts' when she vanished without explanation in the summer of 1966."*

"A recipe book?" Sage straightens. "So, she did write them down, but she didn't get to publish her masterpiece?"

I glance at the tin. "Someone wrote them down." I click on another article, this one from the *Thornhollow Tribune*, dated a few days earlier. *"Local Chef Missing, Foul Play Suspected.* It states that Birdie missed a scheduled dinner at Nottingham, which was completely out of character. When friends checked her home, they found signs of a disturbance but no trace of her."

Rosie shakes her head sadly. "And now we know where she ended up."

"Look at this quote," I point to the screen. *"Birdie's half-sister, Lorna Duval, 27, claims no knowledge of Birmingham's whereabouts. 'I can't believe she would leave me,' Duval told reporters. 'She always took care of me and encouraged me. Said my cooking was as good as hers, if not better, and she wanted the world to know about it.'"*

Rosie frowns. "Lorna established the charity, but I never heard anything about her being a cook."

"Wait a minute." I open a new tab. "If Lorna was 27

when this was written in 1966, she'd be in her eighties now. Does she still live in town?"

Rosie shakes her head. "Not that I know of. She's not on the board for the charity. Is she still alive?"

My fingers fly across the keyboard as I do a search on Lorna. "Found her! Lorna Duval is a resident at Sweet Georgia Pines Nursing Home in Sugar Cove. There's a recent article about her 85th birthday celebration where she —" I pause, reading ahead before sharing, "—attempted to serve her famous peach cobbler to fellow residents. The staff reportedly had to rescue the dessert after it began smoking in the oven. The fire department was called in." I chuckle. "Sounds like that's the real reason the story made the paper."

Sage snorts. "Oh, dear."

"Since she's still alive," Rosie says, "it would be worth talking to her to get the real scoop on Birdie."

The honey pot levitates off the table, then falls. The ceramic breaks into pieces, and honey rolls out over them. We all jump, and my hand flies to my chest. "Goodness, Birdie. There's no need for that."

Kit grabs a dishcloth and begins cleaning up the mess. "You don't have to break things to get our attention." She gives the air a stern look. "Tap once for yes and twice for no." She makes a face as the honey drips from the towel. "Simple and less...sticky."

But what that signifies tugs at me. "Ladies, I think we need to pay Ms. Duval a visit."

Rosie nods. "You guys go. I'll stay here and handle the afternoon appointments."

Sage grabs her bag. "I'm afraid I have to get back to work.

This week is busy with the cookoff tourists coming in." She gives me a look. "They *are* still having the cookoff, right?"

I shut the laptop. I almost forgot about that brewing in the background. "I'll check with Mama, but I assume so?"

Kit tosses out the pieces of the honey pot and rinses the dishcloth in the sink. She glances toward the living room. "What should I do about Caboodle?"

"She can stay here," Rosie says. "I'll keep an eye on her."

She dries her hands. "People love to talk, and I'm a mighty fine listener." She scoops up the cat toys and carries them to the living room, depositing them near the fireplace. "Little old ladies especially love to tell me their stories."

Sage is already at the door and hands me a sachet. "For clarity of mind. Might help Lorna remember."

"Y'all are something else," I say. "Like my own personal supernatural squad."

Rosie laughs, taking her seat at her desk. "And I'll be here making sure your actual business stays afloat while you're off ghost hunting. Again."

"You're a saint," I tell her.

"Your aunt used to run off on ghostly errands, too. Just try to be back by three. The Hostetter party is coming in then, and I'm not about to handle that group alone."

I smile, remembering the woman who taught me everything I know about spirits—and stubbornness. I owe a lot to Aunt Willa.

Caboodle chooses that moment to pounce on a sunbeam dancing across the floor, tumbling head over tiny paws in an explosion of fluff.

"As for this little troublemaker," Rosie says, eyeing the

kitten with mock sternness, "I'm raising two children. One kitten doesn't scare me."

"Famous last words," Kit murmurs, making me snort.

I grab my purse and dig for my car keys. "We shouldn't be long. The nursing home is only about twenty minutes away."

"Take whatever time you need," Rosie assures me. "Just be careful. Between food critics dropping dead and skeletons turning up in trunks, this town's getting weirder by the day."

Chapter Ten

The Sweet Georgia Pines Nursing Home appears to be a perfectly preserved slice of 1982, complete with mint-green wallpaper and dusty silk flower arrangements. As Kit and I push through the glass doors, I'm hit with the unmistakable scent of industrial-strength disinfectant. It barely masks the underlying notes of cafeteria food and talcum powder.

"Smells just like my great-aunt Myrtle's house," Kit whispers, wrinkling her nose. "Minus the seventeen cats."

I hide my grin. Despite the somber reason for our visit, Kit's presence makes even a nursing home feel less intimidating.

The lobby is hushed but not silent. A television murmurs from a corner where two elderly men are locked in what appears to be a decades-long chess rivalry. Somewhere down a hallway, a woman laughs—a bright, unexpected sound in this place where time seems to move differently.

I approach the front desk, where an attendant with kind eyes and box braids pulled into a neat bun glances up from her computer. "Hello," I say, summoning my best small-town politeness smile. "We're here to visit Miss Lorna Duval, if she's accepting visitors."

The attendant wears a name tag that reads Glinda. She taps at her keyboard. "Are you family?"

Kit jumps in smoothly. "We're researching local history. Ms. Duval's half-sister, Birdie Birmingham." She points at me. "Ava here is a judge in this weekend's Thornhollow cookoff, and she's immersing herself in Birdie's legend."

I shoot Kit a grateful look. She's always better at these explanations than I am, probably because psychics are used to talking their way into places where answers might be hiding.

Glinda's face softens. "Oh, Birdie! Lorna talks about her recipes all the time." She lowers her voice. "Between us, I've tried making a few of what Lorna claims are her own versions of those recipes. Bless her heart, that woman couldn't boil water without burning it."

I stifle a laugh. "Is that so?"

"She has a bit of dementia. Been getting worse over the past year. I chalk it up to that." She gestures at the hall to our right. "Room 207. Just past the solarium. She should be in— it's almost time for her afternoon programs."

"Thank you so much," I say, genuinely grateful for her help.

As we make our way down the corridor, I'm struck by how alive the place feels despite its institutional setting. We pass a craft room where elderly hands work diligently on what appears to be a quilt. A therapy dog—a gentle golden retriever with a gray muzzle—pads alongside a volunteer, stopping to collect pets from residents in wheelchairs.

"You know," Kit mutters out of the corner of her mouth, "There's more than just the living in this place. Are you seeing anything...ghostly?"

I resist the urge to roll my eyes. "I don't go looking for them, and neither should you. The last thing either of us needs is a hitchhiker when we leave."

"But this place..." She shivers slightly. "The veil is thin here. Between living and whatever comes next."

I think about Birdie's ghost, wondering if she's with us. "Well, let's focus on the living for the moment. Specifically, Lorna and what she might remember about Birdie."

"If she remembers anything at all. Dementia is tricky, and there might have been some jealousy if Lorna fancied herself a prize cook, too. Tough to live up to a legend."

The corridor stretches before us, doors partially open, offering glimpses of lives condensed to a single room: family photos, crocheted blankets, television screens glowing with daytime game shows.

I pause to let an elderly gentleman with a walker make his way past us. He tips an imaginary hat, and I smile in return.

I stop at room 207, its door adorned with a small whiteboard bearing 'Lorna Duval' in neat script, surrounded by hand-drawn flowers. After exchanging a quick glance with Kit, I rap my knuckles against the door—soft enough not to startle, but firm enough to announce our presence.

After a moment, a soft, lilting voice calls, "Come in?" It's said as a question, as if she's surprised someone's knocking on her door.

We step inside, and there she sits—Lorna Duval, Birdie Birmingham's younger half-sister. The late afternoon sun streams through gauzy curtains, bathing her and a floral armchair by the window in filtered light. Her silver hair is perfectly coiffed, not a strand out of place, and her cardigan matches her slippers with the kind of coordination that speaks of lifelong habits.

I'm startled by the clarity in her eyes as she peers at us. They are bright blue and alert, sparkling with an undisguised curiosity that belies her reported condition. Her gaze sizes us up, taking our measure with the shrewd assessment of a woman who's spent decades navigating the South's inherent social hierarchy.

"May I help you?" She worries a handkerchief stitched in the corners with blue flowers. "Are you from the church?" A slight furrow appears between her brows, then smooths away.

I step forward, offering my warmest smile. "Hello, Ms. Duval. I'm Ava Fantome-Cross, and this is my friend Kit Lyons. We're not from the church—we've come to talk to you about a few things, if you're okay with that."

Her eyes widen, her spine straightens, and a smile blooms across her features. "My goodness," she breathes, one hand fluttering to her neck. "Well, aren't you sweet to come visit. Please, please sit down." She gestures to the pair of chairs opposite her with an elegant sweep of her hand. "It's been ages since anyone's come to talk to me, except those church ladies."

I settle into the chair closest to her, noting the collection of framed photographs on her bedside table—faces from another era, frozen in black and white alongside more recent color snapshots. Kit takes the other seat, her eyes darting around the room in that way she has when she's trying to pick up psychic vibes.

"What can I help you with?" Lorna asks.

Where to start? "I'm curious about your life in Thornhollow." Her chair, worn and sunken, seems to swallow her small frame. "It must have been quite different back then."

Kit wanders over to Lorna's dresser, politely examining more framed photographs, a stack of magazines, and some perfume bottles on a glass tray.

Lorna's eyes drift to the window. "Oh my, Thornhollow was something special. Not like these newfangled towns with their chain restaurants and whatnot." Her voice carries the melodic drawl of old Georgia, each word stretched like taffy. "Daddy owned the general store—Duval's Dry Goods. Everybody came through our doors."

"I didn't know that. Did you work there?"

She straightens a crocheted blanket across her lap. "Yes, of course. I remember the summers most. We'd have peach festivals where the whole town would gather in the square. Mama would dress me up in the prettiest frocks, all ribbons and lace." Pride ripples across her face. "I was runner up for Peach Queen one year, you know."

Her chin lifts a fraction, as if the crown had only narrowly missed her head.

I nod encouragingly, noting how she keeps the conversation firmly in the spotlight of her own memories. Not a whisper about Birdie yet.

"And the Christmas parades!" Her hands become animated. "Daddy would throw candy from his shiny Cadillac. After Mother died, and Daddy remarried, we'd go to the Nottingham Hotel—that's where my stepmother's family made their fortune. They hosted the most elegant holiday parties."

Kit catches my eye from across the room, a subtle head tilt indicating she's found something interesting among the photographs.

I seize on the natural opening. "Speaking of the Birminghams, did you and Birdie spend a lot of time together growing up? I know she was ten years older than you."

The change is subtle but unmistakable. Lorna's smile falters. Her fingers, which had been dancing with her stories, suddenly fall still in her lap. "Birdie?" she repeats, as if testing an unfamiliar word. "Oh, sweet Bernadine..."

Bernadine? "Was that her given name?" I wait, watching as something complicated passes behind her eyes.

"You know, dear," Lorna finally says, her voice dropping an octave, "my memory isn't what it used to be. Birdie was my half-sister, yes, after Daddy remarried. But she was already practically a grown woman at that time." She waves a dismissive hand. "She was nice to me, but we weren't particularly close."

Interesting. I assumed differently from reading the articles. "She was quite the local celebrity with her cooking and storytelling, wasn't she? Do you remember some of that?"

A faraway look enters her eyes. "She did cook a bit. Nothing extraordinary, mind you. Just simple country fare."

Behind Lorna's back, Kit raises an eyebrow. She moves away from the dresser, a silver-framed photograph in her hands. She acts casual, but I recognize the determined set to her mouth. She's found something. "Is this you, Miss Lorna?" she asks, presenting the photo. "My goodness, you were a stunner. And is that Birdie beside you?"

I catch a glimpse of two women standing side by side in front of what must be the old Thornhollow town square. Even in the faded image, the family resemblance is unmistakable.

Lorna reaches for the frame, her arthritic fingers trembling. The moment she touches it, her expression hardens. "Where did you get this? That's private. You shouldn't be going through my things." Her pale eyes dart between Kit and me, suddenly suspicious.

"I'm sorry, ma'am." Kit's voice is gentle. "It was right there on your dresser for all to see."

Lorna clutches the photo to her chest. "She always got everything, but I could cook just as well as she did. That's why she wanted me to help her."

"Help her with what?" I ask.

"She's not here, is she?" Her eyes dart around. "Sometimes I think I see her watching me."

A chill skitters down my spine. Is Lorna sensing Birdie's ghost? Or is this just the ramblings of an older woman with a failing memory?

"Who, Birdie?" Kit asks. "Do you feel her presence, Miss Lorna?"

Lorna doesn't answer. She stares at the window, as if searching for something—or someone—in the garden beyond. The photograph slips from her fingers, landing softly on her lap. "She shouldn't be here," she whispers. "She ran away."

The door opens, and a nurse in a cheerful scrub top enters with a smile that doesn't quite reach her eyes. "I'm sorry to interrupt, but Miss Lorna needs to rest now. How about I turn on your soaps, dear?"

I'm disappointed, but I stand and nod. "Of course. Miss

Duval, thank you so much for your time. We really appreciate you talking with us."

The nurse turns on the TV. Lorna seems barely aware we're leaving, her gaze still fixed on the window.

"Thank you kindly for the visit," Kit adds, gently retrieving the photograph and placing it back on the dresser. "Your stories about Thornhollow were mighty fascinating."

The nurse walks us down the hallway, her rubber-soled shoes making soft squeaking sounds on the polished linoleum. I glance at Kit, who's shooting me a look that says *something ain't right* as clearly as if she'd spoken aloud.

"Nurse—" I pause, reading her name tag, "—Jeffries, has Miss Lorna been a resident here long?"

"Yes, she's been with us over ten years." She nods at one of the ladies using a railing installed along the corridor wall. "Sold her big estate outside Thornhollow when she started having issues living on her own. She moved into a small apartment for a while before ending up here."

Something nudges my brain. "Was the estate in her family long?"

"The Duval property? Oh, heavens, yes. It had been in the family since before the War Between the States." Nurse Jeffries lowers her voice conspiratorially. "She told me she wanted to live out her days there, but there was no one to care for her. All her family was gone."

So sad. "Has she ever talked about her step-sister, Birdie Birmingham?"

The nurse pushes open a door leading to the visitors' lounge. "Miss Lorna talks about Birdie all the time when she's having her good days. She set up a whole charity foundation in Birdie's name after she vanished—the Birdie Birmingham Memorial Fund. You might have heard of it."

"I sure have. She talks about Birdie all the time? But she just acted to us like she barely remembers her."

"That's the dementia." Nurse Jeffries gives a sympathetic smile. "Some days she remembers everything clear as a bell, other days..." She shrugs. "The past gets all mixed up."

Kit chimes in. "Does she talk about Birdie's cooking?"

The nurse chuckles, a warm sound that echoes in the empty corridor. "Lord, yes. Though always with the same comment—that Birdie got all the glory, but Lorna was the real cook in the family. Between you and me" —she lowers her voice again—"the kitchen staff dreads when Miss Lorna insists on 'helping' with the meals, bless her heart."

The classic Southern insult wrapped in sugary politeness—a staple around these parts. "Do you think she was jealous of Birdie's cooking fame?"

"Maybe. Miss Lorna has a scrapbook filled with old articles about Birdie and her dinners. Shows it to anyone who'll look, then claims those recipes were hers."

I think about the cards in the tin. "Hers?"

A nod. "She claims that Birdie stole them. But then she'll turn around and talk for hours about how much she misses her sister and how tragic it was when she vanished. Dementia is a thief, stealing good memories or turning them into lies."

This visit has answered a few questions, but left me with even more. "When she mentions Birdie's disappearance, does she ever offer an idea about what she suspects happened to her?"

"Only when she's having what we call her 'sundowning'

episodes. She gets real agitated in the evenings sometimes, claiming Birdie did it on purpose."

"Did what?" Kit asks.

"Left her. That she was jealous of Lorna and ran off, cutting herself off from the family." She straightens her scrubs. "But again, that's probably just the dementia talking. As close as they seemed to be, I can't imagine Birdie would up and leave her. Can you? Doesn't make sense."

"Thank you so much for talking with us." I shake her hand. "You've been incredibly helpful."

Kit and I make it to the exit, the antiseptic smell giving way to fresh air as the automatic doors slide open. "Well, that was about as clear as mud pie," I say, fishing my car keys from my purse.

Kit lets loose a long-suffering sigh. "Lorna knows more than she's letting on, Ava. I felt it when she looked at that photograph—there was recognition, fear, and something else. Maybe guilt?"

"You think she had something to do with Birdie ending up in the trunk?" I click the unlock button on my key fob.

"I think—" Kit begins, but my phone interrupts her with Mama's custom ringtone.

Georgia On My Mind blasts through the air. I grimace apologetically at Kit and answer. "Hey, Mama, I meant to call you about Donna."

"Avalon, you test me to no end!" Mama's voice is so loud, it forces me to hold the phone away from my ear. "You were there when it happened, and you didn't call me? I had to hear it from Queenie?"

"Yes, Mama, I was there, and it was quite upsetting."

"The whole town's in an uproar! I've got reporters from

the *Tribune* camped outside Town Hall, and I have to hold an emergency press conference in twenty minutes about the cookoff. I need you here yesterday!"

I roll my eyes at Kit, who's trying not to laugh. "Mama, I don't think a press conference is the best idea right now—"

"This isn't a request. We've got to get ahead of this before folks start thinkin' the cookoff is cursed!"

Kit mouths "Too late" and I have to stifle a laugh.

"Fine, Mama. I'm on my way."

"Wear something decent. Not that hideous pink blouse and boring tan khakis. You're the head judge for the event now. You need to look the part."

I glance down at my perfectly respectable blouse and pants. "How do you know what I'm wearing?"

"I know everything. Now hurry!" The line goes dead.

I slide into the driver's seat and drop my head against the steering wheel. "How does she do that? She's not the one with psychic abilities."

Kit buckles her seatbelt. "Your mama doesn't need ESP. She's got something more powerful—a mother's intuition."

"Well, now I have to go to Town Hall for what will undoubtedly be the most mortifying press conference in Thornhollow history. I can already hear the townsfolk whispering in the coffee line tomorrow morning." I groan, starting the engine. "At least Lorna gave us something to think about."

"I respectfully disagree with the nurse about the sundowning episodes." Kit adjusts her seatbelt as I pull out of the parking lot. "People with dementia often remember the distant past more clearly than yesterday."

"But we know Birdie *didn't* leave her. She ended up dead and stuffed in a trunk."

"Leaving can be metaphorical, and I think Lorna knows more about what happened to Birdie than she's letting on."

"I do, too, but she's a dead end for now. I'm curious about that estate sale, though. What if Birdie was murdered and stuffed in the trunk right in the Duval home? I should have taken a picture of the trunk so I could have shown it to her. I didn't put two and two together."

"We can still do it."

"Not with the trunk being at the police station and catalogued as evidence."

Kit snaps her fingers in disappointment. "Right."

"I just hope Mama's press conference doesn't turn into a three-ring circus."

Kit gives me a look that could wilt lettuce. "When has anything your mama organized ever been anything less?"

Chapter Eleven

Two days later, I stare at the dregs of my teacup while Sage settles up with a customer.

She's picked a lovely Victorian flower theme for the month, rows of vintage cups and saucers lining a shelf above her specialty tea blends. Paper flowers adorn the display case, which features a variety of homemade cupcakes, breads, and tarts. Pictures of Victorian ladies having tea are framed on each of the café tables.

Once the woman leaves, Sage drops into the seat across from me with her own cup of brew. Mine is lemon blueberry; hers smells like mint and hibiscus.

"What did the report say?" She's tied her hair back with a yellow scarf that covers much of her forehead. It has tiny rhinestones sewn into it, and they flash under the lights as she moves her head.

Doc put a rush on Donna Dean's autopsy report. Birdie's skeleton has been put on hold. "Amatoxin," I tell her.

Her brows rise, and her eyes go round. "From a mushroom?"

"You know about amatoxins?"

"Enough to stay far away from them." She circles the rim of her cup with a finger. "Death Cap, Destroying Angel—do they know which one? There are others, too, but I'm not as familiar with them. Neither is native to our area, but they're both prevalent in North America and easily confused with nontoxic varieties."

"I didn't get to read the report. You know Jones is keeping me out of the investigation. Doc was kind enough to share a few facts with me, but wasn't comfortable emailing me the entire thing."

"I bet it was Destroying Angel. Eating just one cap can kill an adult, and it works fast."

"Yikes."

"Do they think she ate one by accident?"

I shrug. The tea leaves in my cup resemble a Rorschach test. "I assume so. At least, Jones let Brax go."

"Does he put mushrooms in his cornbread?"

"No, thank goodness. They found none in his kitchen, either. Brax, as we already knew, wasn't the culprit. Since Donna was a foodie, they're chalking her death up to something she ate before she arrived, possibly that breakfast sandwich, but no one knows where it came from. Since there haven't been any other reports in the area of folks being admitted to the hospital or dying from mushroom poisoning, the source is unknown."

"Which points to it be specifically aimed at Donna. What's Detective Jones doing next?"

I glance out the window. A line of cars is filling the

meager parking spots we have. The town has been flooded with reporters, Donna's fans who are holding nightly vigils outside The Honey Bar, and the curious, who simply want to follow a potential scandal. "No clue, but did you see his last media conference? It rivals Mama's from the other day."

"So much gossip swirling about Donna's death and Brax's involvement." Sage clicks her tongue and shakes her head. "At least now, the truth is out."

"Except they have no idea when she consumed the toxin or where. There are no remnants of her last meal. Thankfully, Mama hired Donna's previous recipe developer to take her place with judging."

"Rosie was curious about that. She said Raylene Stokes and Donna didn't exactly trade cookie recipes."

One of the paper flowers falls to the floor. We exchange a glance. "Miss Birdie?" she asks.

I'm not sure if she's asking me or speaking to the ghost. "She's terrorizing my kitchen. I think she's unhappy about my lack of follow-through with her investigation."

"What can you do? Kit said that talking to Lorna got you nowhere, and Jones hasn't been able to look into it, what with this Donna Dean stuff." She glances at the fallen flower. "Of course, a séance is still an option."

"I may take you up on that, but if there's a block around her recipe cards, could there be one around her spirit, too? If so, can she break through it and talk to us?"

Sage purses her lips. "Hmm. Possibly. I still think it's worth a try."

"Well, I've got appointments all afternoon, and tonight I have to attend the dinner for the cookoff judges at the hotel.

They're turning it into a sort of memorial for Donna, too, I guess. Maybe tomorrow?"

"Do you want me to come tonight as backup? Birdie might show up."

"I doubt her spirit can travel that far." Most are locked into an area within five miles of their bones. "But you're welcome to attend if you want. I can use all the moral support I can get."

She pats my arm. "Rosie is going and I'll bring Kit, too. You'll have the full Ava posse ready to spring into action."

I tip my teacup toward her to show her the leaves. "Please tell me this says I'm going to ace this judging gig."

She blinks and isn't quite quick enough to hide her flinch.

"What?" I say, my heart falling.

A grimace. "It's an octopus."

"Okay, and that means...?"

"Are you sure you want to know?"

I sigh. "No, but you better tell me anyway."

"Danger," she says. "An octopus signifies danger."

Another paper flower falls to the floor. I push to my feet. "Just another day in my life."

Later that evening, I lean in to kiss Logan goodbye, catching a whiff of his cologne—a blend of citrus and cedar that always makes me smile. He's hunched over his desk, phone pressed to his ear, but his eyes soften as they meet mine.

"I'll be there soon," he whispers, covering the mouthpiece. "Just gotta wrap up this call with Chuck about the new brewery label designs."

"Don't you dare leave me to fend off Mama's world domination plans all night," I tease, tapping his nose playfully.

He chuckles, his tousled hair sticking up in six different directions. His brother can be a lot. "Wouldn't dream of it. Save me a slice of peach cobbler?"

"You know I will."

As I drive to the Nottingham Hotel, my stomach is tense. This dinner is bound to be quite the affair, especially since we're now turning it into a memorial for Donna as well. The drive through the countryside does me good, though. I leave the window down, even though the wind teases my hair, and it clears my head.

When I round the last bend and see what awaits, however, I cringe. The place is absolutely swarming. Cars line both sides of the road, and I can see a steady stream of people in their Sunday best heading towards the grand old building.

I finally find a spot to park in the overflow field near the lake, the grass tickling my ankles as I step out. The air is thick with the perfume of magnolias and the excited chatter of what seems like half the county.

My stomach twists. This is not my idea of fun. "Donna Dean, you know how to draw a crowd, even in death."

I make my way to the entrance, dodging clusters of gossiping ladies and gentlemen comparing bow ties. The energy is palpable, a strange mix of somber remembrance and barely contained excitement for the upcoming cookoff.

"Ava Cross, as I live and breathe," a familiar voice calls out. Mabel Jansen catches up to me, her hair sprayed into an elegant bun, hustling through the crowd. "Ain't this some-thin'? I haven't seen a turnout like this since Buford Thompson set a church pew on fire during Revival Week in eight-nine."

I nod, a bit overwhelmed. "It's certainly something."

She wipes at the corner of her eye with an embroidered handkerchief. "Donna touched a lot of lives with her cooking, that's for sure."

As we near the entrance, I wonder what secrets and stories are simmering beneath all this Southern charm and hospitality. One thing's for certain—this evening promises to be as rich and complex as Queenie's famous seven-layer dip.

As I step into the hotel's grand foyer, the buzz of conversation washes over me. Before I can squeeze through the nearest group of folks, a familiar voice cuts through the din. "Avalon! There you are!"

Mama, resplendent in a powder blue suit, makes a beeline for me. Her curls are perfectly coiffed, and her smile is wide, but I know that look in her eyes. "Hey, there," I say, bracing myself.

She immediately starts fussing with my hair. "Honey, didn't you check the time? My speech is about to start, and here you are, late as a June bug in July."

I resist the urge to roll my eyes. "I got here as fast as I could, Mama. I do own a business, and we're busy. And the parking lot is a gladiator arena."

"You're here now," she says, scanning the room over my shoulder.

"Where's Daddy?"

"He'll be here any minute. He's going to play a couple of songs at the end of the dinner."

At least that's something to look forward to. My father

became a rock star when I was a young girl. He's given up that life, but he still puts on a show or two for the locals every year.

"There's Raylene," Mama says. "I need to check that there's plenty of dessert before I go on stage. No one expected this big of a turnout! I wish Queenie were here. I know she couldn't get away from the beehive for this, but I sure would feel better if she were in charge." She scans my outfit, her face screwing into a frown. "You go on and find your seat at the judges' table, dear. And do try to look more...judicial."

Before I can ask what 'judicial' is supposed to look like, she's off. "And the whirlwind that is Dixie Fantome strikes again," I mutter to myself.

I make my way to the ballroom. It's a sea of faces, some familiar and others not, all dressed in their finest, their voices creating a low hum of excitement. Many are in somber colors, as if we're attending a wake.

In some ways, I guess we are. Who knew that in Georgia, you can celebrate an upcoming cookoff and mourn a person at the same time?

As I approach the reserved table, my eyes are drawn to the empty chair. A small placard reads "Donna Dean" in elegant script, and a pang of sadness hits me unexpectedly. After nodding at of the other judges, I settle into my seat, running my fingers along the crisp white tablecloth.

Around me, the chatter continues, but I'm so lost in thought that I nearly jump when someone touches my arm. It's Dr. Abernathy, looking dapper in his bow tie, a gentle smile on his face. "Evening, Ava. Quite the turnout, isn't it? I didn't know Ms. Dean, but if she was anything like her reputation, I'd speculate, she'd have loved every bit of this fuss."

I nod, grateful for the friendly face. "Terrible about the poisoning."

He says a quick hello to the other judges and lowers his voice. "I know tonight's dinner is important to the cookoff, but I must admit, I have reservations about eating anything I haven't prepared myself after what happened to her."

His words seem to hold a warning. As he leaves to take his seat, I scan the crowd. Was Donna's death murder? Is the killer here tonight? Before I can dwell on it, the lights dim, and Mama takes the stage, ready to kick off the evening's event.

Her mayoral voice fills the room, her Southern charm turned up to eleven as she welcomes everyone. I'm only half-listening, still scanning the crowd, when I spot two familiar faces slip in through the back doors. Kit and Sage. I catch Sage's eye and wave, feeling a rush of relief at seeing my friends.

As Mama orates about community spirit and the importance of preserving culinary traditions—as if anyone here needs convincing—I notice a steady trickle of people filing past a table in the far rear corner.

"It's a memorial for Donna," Missy Ray, seated next to me, whispers.

A framed photo of Donna's beaming face sits surrounded by candles, and a leather-bound book lies nearby. People pause to write notes in it.

Detective Jones, looking decidedly uncomfortable in a blazer instead of his usual uniform, hovers nearby. He's trying to be subtle, but regards each person who approaches the book with an intense scrutiny. He isn't watching for mourners—he's watching for guilt.

"Well, well, Detective," I murmur, "I didn't expect to see you playing dress-up tonight."

Missy gives me a strange look. I flash her my best 'just talking to myself' smile and turn my attention back to Jones. He's so focused on the memorial table that he doesn't notice me watching him. Part of me wants to march over and demand to know if he actually has any leads. But I know that would only make him clam up. Besides, Mama would have my hide if I caused a scene during her big speech.

So I put on my best judge face, and wonder what secrets might be hidden in that memorial book. And more importantly, what ghosts—literal or figurative—might be haunting this gathering tonight. Of all the times I wish spirits would leave me alone, tonight I'd be relieved if at least one of them, most especially Donna, would appear and tell me how she ingested toxic mushrooms.

Mama gives details about the cookoff and offers a brief introduction of each of us at the table. She also points out Raylene Stokes, the cook in charge of our dinner. Raylene waves at the crowd, and many wave back and applaud.

The tinkling of silverware against china signals the arrival of the first course. Missy, her dark hair a match for her eyes, offers me a smile. "I do declare, Ava, I haven't seen you since the county bakeoff last summer."

I rack my brain, but come up blank. Did I attend the bakeoff? I've been so busy, the days, weeks, and months are a blur. "It has been a while."

I toy with the salad that's delivered by a waiter, Doc's words still circling my brain. A recollection of the bakeoff finally surfaces, along with something my mother said about it. "Mama claimed your blackberry cobbler was divine."

"Not divine enough." Missy's sniff is sharp enough it could slice a peach. She stabs at her salad with unnecessary force. "I still can't believe Donna's mediocre peach crumble took first place. Between you and me, I suspect there was some funny business going on."

Donna was there? I drink some tea, leaving the salad alone. "What do you mean about funny business?"

Missy leans in, holding her fork close to her mouth as if to hide her lips. "Let's just say, I wouldn't put it past Donna to have greased a few palms."

Mama wasn't in charge of the event, but I'm doubtful those who were would take bribes. Still, I process this tidbit and wonder if Missy's lingering resentment might be more than sour grapes. Could it be a motive for something sinister?

Bo Remington clears his throat from the other side of the empty chair. "Donna hasn't had a truly prize-winning recipe since she fired Raylene. Hard to believe Raylene showed up at all, and with Carter, no less."

"Raylene, the cook?" I ask. The petite gal is working her way through the crowd, talking to folks who are diving into their meals. Her face is expressive, and she laughs at someone's comment a few tables away before moving on. A tall, skinny man in a white apron hails her from across the room. She excuses herself from her audience to go to him.

"Yep, Raylene Stokes," Bo says around a bite of bread as he tracks her path to the man. "And that's her partner, Shane Carter." His mouth twists into a grimace. "It's a crying shame what Donna did to those two."

Through the ballroom door, Rosie rushes in. She hurries

to the table where my other friends are seated and waves at me. I smile and turn back to Bo. "What do you mean?"

His voice drops to a conspiratorial level, and he braces one hand on Donna's empty chair to lean his sturdy body toward me. "Those two were the real secrets to Donna's initial success. Her culinary dream team. They made her famous. And now, they've got every reason to want her name off the menu for good."

Missy chimes in. "Back then, Donna was just a loud voice in a crowded kitchen—no real talent, no original ideas —until she hired Raylene as her recipe developer and Shane as her sous chef."

Bo nods in agreement. "Raylene was the creative genius. She could turn a simple biscuit into magic, and a cornbread into a symphony." He gives a sigh as he glances at her. She's directing a waiter to a table that's been missed. "Shane was the hands-on workhorse. Reliable, charming, and able to execute Raylene's ideas flawlessly. Together, they were unstoppable."

I study the couple, my dinner forgotten. Through the crowd, a young woman pushes an older woman in a wheel-chair to the end of our table, where the name placard reads, *Shirley Walker*. Another judge? I return my attention to my companions while the aide gets her settled and a waiter brings her a plate of food. "What happened?"

"Shane," Missy and Bo say in unison.

As if the man feels our attention on him, he turns and glances our way. I quickly avert my gaze, pick up my iced tea, and down a long drink. "What about him?" I ask behind my glass.

Missy attacks her salad again. "Donna nursed a long-simmering crush on him, but when she realized his heart belonged to Raylene, her jealousy curdled into something bitter and vindictive. She fired them both, claiming they were stealing her recipes and undermining her brand."

Bo straightens and shoves his salad plate aside. "To ensure they couldn't compete with her, Donna used her blog to tarnish their reputation." He shakes his head in disgust. "She wrote scathing reviews of their restaurant, Southern Comforts, accusing them of theft, poor hygiene, and even serving spoiled food. Within months, they lost everything, including their reputation and their livelihood. Like I said, they're the last folks I'd expect to see here."

Missy swallows and waves her fork in the air. "Raylene took catering gigs. Shane washed dishes. They watched Donna thrive off their recipes, getting book deals, TV appearances, and sponsorships, while they scraped by. Such a shame."

"Yes," I say, "that is a shame." And a motive for murder. At the memorial table, a scuffle has broken out. A man in jeans and a T-shirt is arguing with a woman. I can't hear what they're saying, but Jones steps in and breaks it up. The man whips around, his face a storm cloud. He stomps through the tables to the exit. Something about him seems familiar, yet I'm sure I don't know him.

"That's Donna's ex, Justin Bowles," Bo tells me. "What a creep. Another chink in Donna's long line of enemies. Didn't expect to see him here either."

Does everyone tied to Donna carry a grudge or a secret? "If you'll excuse me..."

I leave my seat, intent on approaching Raylene and Shane, but a gentle hand catches my wrist as I pass the end of the table. The older woman in the wheelchair smiles up at me.

"I don't believe we've met." Her silver hair gleams in the soft light of the ballroom. "I'm Shirley Walker. Your mama was kind enough to invite me tonight as an honorary judge."

A gentle charm radiates from her. "Miss Shirley, it's a pleasure."

The seat nearest her is empty, but I see her aide carrying a tray toward us. Someone hails her, and she pauses to chat with them.

Shirley keeps her grip on my wrist. "I heard you've been asking about dear Birdie. Lord, the stories I could tell you about that woman."

My pulse skips. "You knew Ms. Birmingham?"

"Knew her?" Shirley chuckles. "Why, we were thicker than thieves back in the day. Sit with me a spell. I'll tell you all about her."

This is too good to pass up. As if summoned by fate, or perhaps something more ghostly, I find myself talking to the one person in the room who might hold the keys to Birdie's past.

I grab Donna's empty chair and pull it up to sit next to Shirley. Hopefully, taking the dead woman's seat is not a faux pas. I'm sure Mama will let me have it later if it is. "Do tell," I say.

Chapter Twelve

As I settle in, Shirley's face grows wistful. "Birdie was a force of nature, that's for sure. She believed in people, you know? Always told me I had talent and needed to leave this town and do something with my life."

"What kind of talent?"

"I was a dancer." Her face is radiant. "Tap dance. I felt so free when I was lost in the music and the movement."

"And did you leave?"

Her thin fingers fiddle with her napkin. "I went to Atlanta a few times to audition for different things, but nothing came of it. I ended up marrying and raising a family in Gainesville. I thought about Birdie every day. Sure wish she would have stuck around."

"Do you know where she went?"

Shirley shakes her head, her fingers continuing to work over her napkin, folding and re-folding it. "No idea. Every birthday, every Christmas, I kept thinking she would send me a note. A letter. A card. *Something*. She never did. It was so unlike her. I know I wasn't the only one who felt like she just abandoned us. Her poor sister went into a terrible funk after Birdie left."

"Any idea why she would do that? Just pick up and leave all of you?"

Shirley clucks her tongue. "She never did get along with her stepdaddy or Lorna. She tried her best, but it was like oil and water with them, and her mama would never take her side about anything. Her mama doted on Lorna, and there was enough of an age discrepancy between the two girls, they had nothing in common."

"Not even cooking?"

"When Lorna got old enough, she thought she could out-cook Birdie, bless her heart. But that was a joke."

I chuckle. This confirms what the nurse told me. "Was Lorna jealous of her big sister?"

"Jealous doesn't even begin to cover it." Shirley sighs. "But let me tell you something sweet about Birdie. Her daddy used to draw the most beautiful birds in her recipe notebooks."

My breath catches. The illustrations on the recipe cards flash through my mind. "She kept notebooks of recipes?"

Shirley nods, her eyes misting over. "Oh yes, with little bluebirds in the margins. He said it was to remind Birdie of her name, and that she could always fly free."

Those recipe cards, with their delicate bird drawings, suddenly mean so much more. "I thought she never wrote any of her recipes down."

"She had trouble with reading. What do they call it these days? Where you mix up some of your letters?"

"Dyslexia?"

She pats my arm. "That's it. Back then, no one understood it, so she kept many things in her head. Writing them down didn't do much good. Recipes were a bit different for her. Different from, say, reading a fiction story. They seemed to help her organize her thoughts, but she was always worried that Lorna or someone else would steal them. She worked hard on printing them. Poor thing never could do cursive. Said it looked like cooked spaghetti to her. But those recipes, and her little ghost stories, were all she had. They made her who she was."

"She only printed things out?"

A nod. "Our teachers back then were hard on her about it, too. They didn't understand about learning disabilities back then."

"About those ghost stories, did she just make those up?"

Shirley chuckles. "They were for real. Most people thought she made them up to add a layer of intrigue to her recipes, but she could see them. Spirits." She gives an emphatic nod. "She saw ghosts."

"You don't say?" A deeper connection to her settles deep in my chest. "Where do you think she went?"

"She was having a fling with this man named Chester. Chester Livingston. He was a two-bit con man from up Chicago way. He promised to take her to the big city and put her recipes in a book. He liked the ghost story angle, thought she could capitalize on both those stories and her delicious cooking. They were going to start with a cookbook and then open restaurants all throughout the South. Lord, she talked about that dream for months. I knew that man was no good, but she couldn't see it. She was head over heels for him."

"And you believe she ran off with him? What do you think happened?"

"Same thing that always happens with men like that—he promised her the moon, then delivered nothing but heartache. She probably ended up barefoot and pregnant, too ashamed to come back and admit she failed."

"Did the police investigate him?"

She fiddles with her napkin more. "They claim they did, but you know how it was back then. A black woman disappeared, chasing after some guy. In my opinion, they didn't take it too seriously. There are days when I wish I had done more. That *I* had gone after her, tried to find her. It's one of the biggest regrets of my life."

Now it's my turn to pat her arm. "You had no way of knowing where she was or what was going on." *Or the fact that she was dead and stuffed in a trunk.* "Did you stay in touch with Lorna after it happened?"

"I tried, but that girl got on my last nerve. You ask me, I think some of her funk was just a cover. She liked getting attention, and after Birdie disappeared, she made the most of it. First, as the shocked sister whom Birdie abandoned. Once she beat that angle to death, she tried to step into Birdie's shoes and take over with the secret dinner clubs. She might as well have nailed Jell-O to a tree. I think she only held one or two before it dawned on her that no one was interested in her dishes."

"It was a sweet gesture for Lorna to create the charity in Birdie's name, though."

Her expression turns wistful again. "Seemed to me like she was trying to put Birdie's ghost to rest."

My pulse skips. "What do you mean?"

She blinks and glances at me. "She needed closure. She never knew what happened to her sister, and I guess, we never will. She had all of Birdie's things cluttering her house, and she held a big estate sale, getting rid of most of it. I remember because I came to look for the old cedar trunk that Birdie always loved. Her daddy built it for her. That thing weighed as much as an elephant." She chuckles. "Birdie kept all of her precious things in it. Those notebooks her daddy gave her, some trinkets she had from admirers, and pictures of some of her role models. I'm sure it devastated her to leave it behind. Why, I remember she had this giant book by Julia Child. She struggled to read it, but she pored over the recipes, saying she was going to create her own master cookbook someday. Of course, hers would be about Southern cooking, not French." Sadness seeps into her voice. "Oh, Birdie, I wish you had realized all your dreams."

The glass of tea on the table in front of her trembles. She doesn't notice, but I do. Goosebumps race over my arms. *Apparently, Birdie can travel beyond the five-mile limit from her bones.*

Shirley's aide arrives at the table and sets down the platter, introducing herself. We exchange a few pleasantries about the food and the event, and she goes on and on about what a generous person my mama is for inviting Miss Shirley to be an honorary judge. I wholeheartedly agree. I gently touch Shirley's hand. "Thank you for sharing all this with me. It means more than you know."

She gives me that charming smile. "Of course, dear. I'll see you at the cookoff on Saturday?"

"You surely will."

I spot Logan's familiar tousled hair across the room. He

catches my eye and grins. I excuse myself and make my way to him. He's chatting with Rosie, Kit, and Sage.

"Hey, y'all." I give Logan a quick peck on the cheek. "I've got some news about Birdie, but first, I need to talk to someone."

Logan puts an arm around my shoulders. "Did you even eat?"

My stomach growls. "What do you say we hit the pizza joint on the way home?"

Rosie scoffs. "Pizza over this fine cooking? Are you crazy? Raylene and Shane are the best. It's amazing that Baldwin and Kalina were able to get them for tonight on such short notice."

"The jury is still out on the level of my insanity," I joke. I gaze toward Raylene and Shane, planning to talk to them first before I snag Detective Jones and tell him all I've learned. "You know them?"

"*Of* them," she corrects. "After their diner went bankrupt, they pivoted and started offering services to hotels and event planners."

"We've never used them, have we?" I ask.

"You know Queenie gets the majority of our business. The few times she's been booked, they were booked, too."

"I'm in for the pizza stop," Sage says. "But I've got to be back at the shop before nine so I can prep for tomorrow. It's going to be another big day."

Kit sighs. "I'll pass. Gotta get home to Caboodle and see how much damage she's done."

Rosie swipes on a fresh coat of lipstick and checks her phone for messages. Her hubby must be home with their kids. "You need a cat kennel for her when you're not there."

"I do, but I haven't had time to go to the store," Kit admits. "So far, I've been keeping her locked in the bathroom. I kitty proofed it, and yet, that cat has managed to scratch up the vanity, chew up a rug, and pee in the bathtub."

We all chuckle. Mama's voice booms through the speakers. "Ladies and gentlemen, if I could have your attention for just a moment..."

I groan inwardly. "Oh lord, here we go again."

She launches into another speech about the cookoff, reminding everyone that it is still on and will begin on Friday evening with the appetizers category, and run into Saturday with the rest.

The lights suddenly flicker. Folks gasp and look up at the giant chandeliers with concern. They flicker again, and I instinctively grab Logan's arm.

Then, as if choreographed by invisible spirits, every plate in the ballroom begins to rise. Mashed potatoes, green bean casserole, and slices of honey-glazed ham hover in mid-air like a squadron of Southern cuisine UFOs.

"What in the world?" Logan mutters.

I back toward the wall but get nowhere when I run into a table. "This can't be good."

In the next breath, the airborne dishes zoom across the room, pelting guests with their contents. Cries echo through the room, and women scream. A glob of sweet potato soufflé splatters against Kit's cheek, while a dinner roll bounces off Sage's forehead.

"Duck!" I yell, pulling Logan down as a gravy boat sails over our heads.

The ballroom erupts into chaos. A lady shrieks as

creamed corn rains down on her carefully coiffed hair and dry-clean-only dress. A man in a seersucker suit scrambles for cover, using serving trays as a makeshift shield.

As we crawl under a table, I call under my breath. "Birdie? Donna? If this is either of you, knock it off!"

Chapter Thirteen

The ballroom looks like a food tornado hit it. Gravy splatters the walls, mashed potatoes cling to the curtains, and jalapeno poppers dangle from the chandeliers. Guests stand shell-shocked, dripping with various Southern delicacies.

Kit, Sage, and Rosie have escaped the worst of it. Logan and I are moderately unscathed as well.

Baldwin and Kalina dash about in a frenzy. Baldwin shouts, his hair plastered to his forehead with a glob of dressing, "Ladies and gentlemen, please remain calm! We assure you, this is all part of our...er...interactive dining experience!"

Kalina nods vigorously, her silk tank top askew and covered with dark splotches. "Yes, yes! A taste of true Southern hospitality...quite literally!" She forces a laugh that sounds more like a strangled hiccup.

Kit snorts. "Way to spin it."

Sage shakes her head and pulls out one of her bottled sprays, misting the air around us with her signature herbal blend for warding off evil spirits. "Was that Birdie? Donna? Someone else?"

I shrug. "I couldn't see anyone."

"Interactive dining experience, my foot!" a stout gentleman in a now-ruined suit bellows. "I demand compensation for this outrage!"

"Oh, hush, Harold," his wife chides, scraping lettuce off her shoulder. "This is the most excitement we've had in years! Reminds me of cousin Earlene's wedding. Now that was a food fight!"

Sage moves toward Kalina. "I'm going to help them clean up."

"Me, too," Rosie says, appearing beside me. "This is going to take a lot of Windex."

Kit checks her phone. "I gotta run. Caboodle's already been alone for two hours. Lord only knows what she's managed to do."

As they all leave, I glance around, noting the mix of outrage and amusement on faces. An elderly lady near me leans in, whispering conspiratorially, "You know, I've always heard this place was haunted. Guess the ghostly guests decided to spice things up a bit, eh?"

Ruining good food doesn't seem like Birdie's style. Could it be Donna's? She probably doesn't like Raylene and Shane catering the event.

A glance toward the memorial table reveals that it's been turned upside down, the candles extinguished, their jars broken. The book lies tattered under the vase of roses, which were dumped on the floor, water and all.

"This is unacceptable!" A woman in a white pantsuit— now more tea-colored than anything—stomps toward

Baldwin and Kalina. "I came here for a high-end meal, not to be assaulted by flying fried chicken!"

Mama hurries over. "Well, that suit should have stayed in your closet until after Memorial Day, dear. Remember the rule about wearing white? Not before Memorial Day and not after Labor Day." She pats her arm as the woman stutters. "I'm sure the hotel will pay your dry-cleaning bill."

This is going to be a PR nightmare. At least my mother looks relatively unscathed. I scan the crowd but see no sign of the detective. Daddy has arrived, though, and glances around, his guitar case in hand, looking utterly stunned. Mama rushes over to intercept him.

I tug on Logan's sleeve, pulling him through the throng of bewildered guests. "Come on."

Logan, plucking a smashed olive from off his dinner jacket, follows without question. I can see the wheels turning in that lawyer brain of his, no doubt calculating the liability issues of spectral food fights.

We approach Raylene and Shane where they're huddled together. Raylene is whispering and gesticulating wildly.

I plaster on my sweetest smile. "Well, if it isn't the dynamic duo of the culinary world! Y'all sure know how to liven up a hotel opening."

Her head snaps up, and I note that she is miraculously untouched by the food fight. Her voice is soft but tense. "Sorry?"

"Ava Fantome-Cross." I offer my hand. "I'm one of the cookoff judges. Bo and Missy pointed you out to me and told me about how awful Donna was to you." I tut. "I didn't realize how cutthroat the culinary world is."

"Such a tragedy, what happened to her," Raylene says, but it seems...perfunctory rather than sincere.

Shane's eyes narrow, reminding me of Moxley when he's sussing out a potential treat. "You're a judge?"

Apparently, Mama is right—I don't look judicial enough, and Shane must have been in the kitchen when Mama listed off our names. "It's my first time," I admit with a grimace. "I sort of got roped into it."

I introduce Logan, and they all exchange a round of handshakes. "Must've been hard, competing with Donna," he says, picking up on my line of questioning without me even telling him about what I heard.

To my surprise, Raylene lets out a tinkling laugh. "Oh, honey, Donna wasn't competition. She was an inspiration! That woman could make a bowl of instant grits sound like a gourmet meal."

"Really?" I try to sound curious rather than accusatory. "I heard there might've been some bad blood between you."

Shane shakes his head, his smile as smooth as butter. "Donna was a firecracker, sure, but she was unique. We came here this weekend to—"

Raylene elbows him sharply, cutting off his words. "To help out Baldwin and Kalina, and we sure are sad about Donna's demise. She gave us our start and we are forever grateful to her."

Mama always says, *the sweetest peach often has the biggest pit.* "I'm sure Donna would be touched to know how fondly you remember her." I point at the logo on Shayne's shirt peeking out from his apron. "Is that a good place to eat?"

He rubs a thumb over the words *Forage Diner.* "It was

back in the day. It was our first place. Now, we just do events."

Raylene's face brightens. "Oh, and we're working on a cookbook! It's gonna be a real treasure trove of Southern comfort food."

Shane puts an arm around her. "All the proceeds are going to the Birdie Birmingham Charity. It's our way of honoring that culinary legend. That's why we wanted to attend the cookoff."

"She's my inspiration," Raylene gushes.

Logan's lips quirk. "Sounds like you two should be judges. I'm sure Ava would give up her seat to one of you."

I give him a look. Mama will give us both grief if either volunteers to do that. "The Birdie Charity? That's wonderful. How did you come up with that idea?"

Raylene's smile turns nostalgic. "Lorna, Birdie's sister, provided us with some of Birdie's original recipes. It's like having a little piece of history right in our hands."

I struggle to keep a poker face. Lorna? The same Lorna who's been living in a nursing home with dementia? "Are they handwritten?"

Raylene gives me an odd expression. "Yes, she has beautiful old-fashioned script. You don't see that much anymore."

The pieces of this puzzle keep changing shape. "Well, that's quite a contribution. I'm sure those recipes are worth their weight in gold. I didn't realize Lorna had any of them. Rumor has it that Birdie didn't write her recipes down."

Raylene winks. "I guess Lorna and Birdie were planning on writing a cookbook together, so Lorna had a stash of them. She had them hidden away for years, not knowing what to do with them. Now that she's getting up there in years, she wants to make sure the world gets to have them."

My pulse picks up. "Do they have ghost stories on the backs?"

Raylene blinks, giving Shane a questioning glance. Shane furrows his brow. "Ghost stories?" he echoes.

What do you want to bet that those recipes are not Birdie's? They're Lorna's. "You're testing all of them before you put them in the cookbook, right?"

"Of course," Raylene says, confused by my questions. "All good cooks test their product first."

A man near the lobby desk catches my eye. Jones. I tug on Logan's arm again. "We'd best get going. It was nice to meet you."

The lobby's a mess of soggy guests and harried staff. "What was that all about?" Logan asks.

"Something's not adding up."

"Besides the fact that we just experienced a ghostly food fight?"

Jones disappears behind a group gathered near the wide staircase that leads to the second floor. Younger folks are taking selfies and pointing to their food-encrusted hair and clothes. Donna's ex is holding a mini-press conference, declaring this whole memorial service is a sham. That Donna would have hated it. That the two of them had plans to get back together, and now some wretched human being has ended her life, and the local yokels have nothing to catch her killer. He's saying all of this into his phone. I assume he's live on a social media app, playing it up for likes and hearts.

My stomach sours at his shameless exploitation. "Raylene and Shane are talking about Donna like she was their best friend, but Bo and Missy painted a whole different picture. And the recipes...something just isn't right."

Logan quirks a brow. "Maybe Bo and Missy are spreading gossip."

It's possible, but my gut says no. "The thing about the recipes, though. The handwriting—"

My sentence is cut short as a figure looms in front of us—Detective Jones, looking about as cheerful as a wet cat, blocks our path.

"Fantome." He jerks a thumb over his shoulder in the direction of the ballroom. "You wanna tell me what happened in there?"

"You were there. You saw what happened."

His expression turns into a glower. "You're gonna tell me that was spirits?"

"What else would it be?"

"A couple of hippie hotel owners trying to be cute and get more publicity for this old place."

Arguing with him is pointless. "I saw you watching the people signing Donna's memorial book. Looking for a suspect in her murder? Her ex looks like a winner to me."

He glances at Justin. "It's possible she *accidentally* ingested that mushroom, you know. It's easily confused with others that are non-toxic."

My mind flashes to her body sprawled on the diner floor. My stomach twists. "Seems to me she has plenty of enemies. Maybe you should be interviewing some of them."

"Like who?" he asks, but he doesn't seem surprised at the statement. "I suppose your investigation is proving more successful than mine."

There's an accusation there. I don't deny that I'm delving

into it. "Start with Raylene Stokes and Shane Carter." I gesture at Justin. "Him, too. You don't seriously buy all that *we were getting back together* mumbo jumbo, do you?"

Jones' eyes narrow. "So, which is it, Fantome? Raylene? Shane? Or that guy?" He cocks his chin to the showman, who now has a gathering of folks listening and agreeing with him. Bo Remington says something to him, but Justin waves him off.

I give Jones the lowdown on what Bo and Missy told me, and my surprise at the fact that Raylene and Shane had nothing but good things to say about Donna. "They painted quite a different picture from Missy and Bo. Don't you think that's odd? Like they're trying to hide something?"

Jones grunts, not bothering to pull out his trusty notebook. Maybe he's not carrying it, but I doubt it. "Anything else you'd like to share?"

"About them? No." I don't see any sense in bringing up the cookbook or Birdie's recipes just yet. "But Shirley, the honorary judge, had some interesting things to tell me about Birdie." Maybe I need to talk to Shirley again. "By the way, when will the autopsy on Birdie's skeleton be done?"

"You've already determined that it's Birdie Birmingham? Based on what?"

Logan squeezes my hand, a warning. I squeeze back, assuring him I'm not going to implicate us about the tin. I tap my temple. "You know that I have my sources, Detective. Very reliable, albeit slightly transparent ones."

Jones' frown deepens, clearly not appreciating my ghostly humor. "I need hard evidence, not garbage. I suggest you leave the investigating to the professionals. Good evening."

I can't resist one last parting shot. "Just you wait, Detective. Soon enough, you'll be eating your words. Maybe even a slice of Birdie's famous blessing pie!"

Jones stops in his tracks, his broad shoulders tensing. He turns back to me, his expression filled with exasperation and reluctant curiosity. For a split second, I wonder if he's starting to believe me. "Mrs. Cross, your enthusiasm for this case is noted, but I hope you understand that I need more than"—he makes a rippling gesture with his fingers at the air between us—"ghostly whispers to proceed."

At least he used my married name, although *Mrs. Cross* makes me cringe. That's Helen, my mother-in-law, and I'm lucky she's busy with the vineyard and isn't here tonight. "Of course, Detective."

He eyes me suspiciously, clearly not buying my cooperative act. The silence is broken by those around us, yet his pause goes on several beats longer than is comfortable. "The official investigation is sidetracked but not dead. I've obtained a DNA sample from Lorna Duval to compare with the skeleton's."

I'm shocked by his candor. This is exactly what I've been waiting for. "Oh, that's perfect! I'm sure it'll be a match."

"Uh-huh," he grunts, clearly unconvinced. "We'll see what the DNA says. In the meantime, try not to stir up any more ghostly food fights."

As he marches away, my tongue gets the better of me. "Can't promise that. You know how spirits can be when they're hangry!"

At that moment, Justin's voice rings out like a gunshot. "That's her. She's the one."

All eyes shift to me as he points a finger my way and holds his phone higher.

"Um. What is he talking about?" I whisper to Logan.

"Maybe it's time to leave," he says.

Justin isn't done, though. "She was in the diner, sitting right next to Donna before she ate that casserole. The owner of that dive is her friend. All rather obvious, isn't it? She didn't want Donna taking the spotlight from her, the mayor's daughter, who doesn't have a lick of culinary education or experience." He turns the camera back on himself. "You know what she is? A *wedding gown designer*."

Those watching him, even the ones who know me, tilt their heads and whisper behind their hands.

"She doesn't know the first thing about judging a cookoff, but she now has top billing since she killed Donna."

Logan holds up a hand, anger radiating off of him. "Now, wait just a minute there. That's slander, and making such accusations—"

Justin sneers. "Of course, her lawyer husband steps in to defend her. Is it any wonder justice isn't being done? She's got everyone in this town protecting her. But we won't stand for it! Will we?"

Logan has years of practice at keeping anger under wraps, but when it comes to me, he's naturally protective, and Justin's accusations light a fire in him. "You're skating dangerously close to defamation, Mr. Bowles."

Jones stops Logan before my husband can cross the expanse and rip the phone from Justin's hand. Or punch him. Maybe both. "I've got this," the detective says. "Y'all get out of here."

I grab Logan's arm and tug him after me, dread tumbling around in the pit of my stomach.

Chapter Fourteen

Steam swirls around us, a misty dance partner to the twang of bluegrass sneaking in from the playlist coming from my phone perched on the bathroom counter. Logan is showering with me.

I scrub at my hair, which smells faintly of dill and vinegar, remnants of the spectral food fight that turned dinner into a spectacle. "If I find one more gherkin in my hair, I'm going to turn into a pickle."

He chuckles, that deep, rich sound that makes me smile. "At least you're sweet." His hands replace mine, working shampoo through the tangles with gentle efficiency. Logan Cross III may be a lawyer by day, but right now, he's my personal hairdresser. He's also annoyingly good at it.

I still smack his arm good-naturedly. "Sweet?" I tilt my head back to rinse out the suds. "You're the sweet one. With those blue eyes and that classic nose, you're the picture of Southern good looks, charm, and chivalry."

"Chivalry, huh?" He sluices water over my head. "That

must be why I'm not running from your pickle-scented *eau de parfum*."

I smack him harder this time. "Southern charm won't save you, if you keep that up," I warn, although the grin on my face betrays any attempt at seriousness. We share a laugh, the kind that fills up the room and pushes away any lingering ghostly gloom.

The chime of my phone interrupts the music and disrupts our playful banter. Done with our scrub, we wrap up and towels. I drip onto the tile as I check the screen. It's Brax. *Backyard meeting. ASAP.*

"Seems like there's no rest for the wicked—or the haunted," Logan says, drying his hair as I show him the message.

"Or for lawyers who associate with either," I add.

We finish drying off quickly, moving in tandem as if it's a race to get dressed. He slips into jeans and a faded Cross Winery tee, while I opt for a comfortable sundress that whispers against my skin in the cool air-conditioning.

He reaches for my hand to lead me out to the back porch. "Ready?"

I slide into flip-flops and nudge Moxley aside as I accept his hand. The dog keeps sniffing me as if I'm his next meal.

Stepping out into the backyard a minute later, the warm evening air mimics the humidity of our shower. A symphony of early summer cicadas fills the twilight, their song punctuated by the occasional croak of a frog from the nearby stream.

Down the long hill by that stream, Tabitha sits with her feet in the water. She's in human form and has donned clothes. My grandfather, a ghost, stands a few feet away, skipping rocks while she watches. He waves. She glances over her shoulder at us.

"Odd that you haven't seen Persephone since you found the skeleton," Logan says. "Isn't it?"

Does my guardian know something? Is she avoiding me on purpose? I wave back at my grandfather and gaze across the yard, where the familiar hedge line draws a neat green border between our little slice of heaven and the bed-and-breakfast. The faintest scent of Carolina jasmine tiptoes on the breeze, mingling with the earthy aroma of freshly watered soil. "She loves to drop ghost bombs and run," I remind him.

"Yoo-hoo! Ava, Logan!" Rhys' voice sails over the hedge, as if he's calling out bingo numbers at the county fair.

"Hey." I wave a hand above the shrubbery. We recently had the overgrown boxwoods trimmed. "Is everything okay?"

Logan's arm slips around my waist as we push between the stately bushes. We amble over to our friends, who are both in casual pants and shirts. Behind them, the B&B lights glow from all the windows.

"Better now," Brax says.

Logan juts his chin to their house. "How's business?"

"We're packed," Rhys says.

I bat away a pesky gnat. "Brax, I'm so glad you've been cleared of suspicion."

He issues a big sigh. "Thanks to your husband."

I nudge Logan. "I reckon that's cause for celebration, don't you think?"

"I suppose it is," Logan agrees, his smirk audible in his voice.

Brax's expression is one of relieved bemusement. "Well, I wouldn't exactly say I'm free. Jones told me not to leave town, but I did want to say thank you."

The stars are out, and a breeze tickles my cheeks. I still smell like relish. I wave away Brax's concern and appreciation. "Anything for you. And Jones is about as subtle as a bull in a china shop when it comes to giving orders. His crime scene techs didn't find any of the mushrooms in the cornbread dressing or in your restaurant. He doesn't have the evidence he's always demanding is critical to convicting a suspect."

"Doesn't mean he's letting me off the hook." Brax's worry lines ease into a smile. "That man loves to throw his weight around."

"And there's a considerable lot of it," Logan says, offhandedly, making all of us chuckle.

"Anyway, it's nice not to be the prime suspect anymore," Brax says. "Now, if only we could figure out what's really going on."

"I'm working on it," I assure him. "I heard some interesting gossip tonight at the dinner about some folks who have every reason to want revenge on Donna."

Rhys flaps a hand in the air. "OMG, we heard about a food fight. Kit texted me and said it was supernatural. Is that true?"

Logan keeps his hand on my lower back. "You should've seen it, invisible hands whipping mashed potatoes and flinging biscuits like frisbees."

"Wait a minute." Rhys' eyes are wide with mischief. "Are you telling me there was indeed an actual food fight with ghosts?"

"Sure was," I reply. "One second, folks are spilling the tea, and the next, it's a full-blown brawl. I swear, Donna's spirit was stirring the pot—literally."

"And she left us smelling like a pickle jar." Logan shakes his head as if he still can't quite believe what we witnessed. "Ava was dodging dinner rolls like a pro."

"Pickles. That's what that odor is," Brax says with a grin.

"Was it really Donna?" Rhys edges closer, the flicker of curiosity lighting up his face. "You saw her?"

I shrug, fiddling with my still-wet hair. "No, but I think she's upset about her untimely death, and her killer might have been there tonight."

Brax frowns. "Too bad she didn't put her skills to better use and point him out to you."

"Ghosts are rarely helpful like that. I think Birdie might've been in on the action, too. I found out some revealing things about her."

Rhys rubs his hands together. "Do tell. I want to hear all about her, back from the beyond, flinging her famous blessing pie across the room."

Logan laughs. "Sure beats rattling chains and moaning through the walls. And she did throw her recipe tin around at The Honey Bar, right?"

The memory brings back another on its heels. A man's face. Excitement races through me, and I snap my fingers. "That's how I know him."

"Who?" Logan says.

"Justin Bowles. I thought he looked familiar, but it's only because I saw him at The Honey Bar. He was peering in the window when Donna came strutting in and put on that show for us."

Rhys, with that mischievous glint in his eye that usually precedes a bombshell, lowers his voice to a conspiratorial level. "Her ex?"

"The very one."

Rhys pulls out his phone and taps the screen before showing it to me. "Did you know Donna was writing an exposé on food frauds? It turns out her ex is one of them. The news went viral while you were at the dinner. I wish I could have been there."

The photo is a publicity shot of Justin in a chef's hat and apron, grinning for the camera. "That's him. He was watching Donna flirt with you." I point to Brax.

Rhys drops his hand and gives Brax the evil eye. "She was flirting with you?"

Brax frowns at me. "Ava is exaggerating. It was nothing."

I remove my foot from my mouth. "You know how those types are, always overdoing the drama for the camera."

"Mmm hmm," Rhys says, still giving Brax the look usually reserved for people who double dip the salsa.

Logan whistles, low and long. "Food fraud is sacrilege around these parts. If she named names..." He trails off, but we all understand what he means.

"Exactly," Rhys nods. "That's motive if I've ever heard one." He pockets his phone. "And some of the cooks who were on Donna's radar are apparently freaking out about it. Her agent and publicist have both issued statements in the past hour. The book is being put on hold until they can verify what she wrote, and the mystery around her death is solved."

The jovial atmosphere takes a backseat to the brewing storm of these implications. Inside the house, Moxley barks once. Probably one of the cats is tormenting him again. I tap a finger on my chin. "Donna might have stirred up more than just controversy with that exposé. The irony is, she was a fraud herself."

All three men look at me. I give them the lowdown on Raylene and Shane, finishing with, "She was using them to build her brand and not giving them the credit for it. Her crush on Shane led to her firing them and then destroying their business. It's terrible what she did."

"Nothing was ever said about that," Brax insists. "Who did she hire to take their places, because, obviously, it must have also been someone capable of making her look good."

Rhys is full of more scandal. "Justin had his own blog and video series when they met. I bet he helped her behind the scenes in more ways than one." He winks.

My mind buzzes. The pieces of the puzzle are dancing just out of reach. Sleep won't come easily tonight—not with phantoms and frauds haunting my thoughts.

I spot movement out of the corner of my eye and glance at the house. There's nothing out of the norm, and I focus on Justin again. "Do you think he was stalking her? Maybe that's why he stayed outside The Honey Bar and was just watching her."

Rhys nods. "If he feared something in that exposé, absolutely. Donna frequently badmouthed him on her blog. That alone might make him want to kill her."

Logan and I exchange glances. "You better mention that you spotted him at the diner right before Donna died to Jones," he tells me.

He's right. I clap my hands together as a signal that our backyard conference under the Georgia stars is adjourning. "I'm off to call our least favorite detective."

"Night, you two," Brax says with a note of concern.

Rhys tips an imaginary hat our way. "Sleep tight, don't let the bed haints bite."

Haints are old-school Southern ghosts who don't simply rattle chains, they mess with your luck. "Only if they promise not to start another food fight," Logan retorts, and we share a collective laugh before parting ways.

I wave goodbye, their silhouettes blurring into the night as Logan and I head back into the sanctuary of our home. Samuel and Tabitha have disappeared into the farmhouse.

The screen door creaks in protest as we step inside, the coolness of the kitchen tiles a welcome contrast to the humidity. Moxley sits by the mudroom door, his sad eyes pinned on the interior of the kitchen. We move in tandem towards the fridge, me reaching for the pitcher of sweet tea while Logan grabs glasses from the cabinet.

"Can you believe all that?" I ask, pouring both glasses. "An exposé gone viral when it hasn't even been published yet. Truth really is stranger than fiction."

"Stranger and more dangerous," Logan concurs, leaning back against the counter, sipping his tea contemplatively. "You need to tread carefully, Ava. That exposé could have ruffled some very real feathers. Silencing Donna after it was written seems illogical, but stranger things and all that."

I set my glass down with a decisive thud. "Guess I better call Jones."

The kitchen has grown dark. Logan moves to the wall to turn on the overhead light. "I'll look into any legal actions that may have come from Donna's culinary crusades. There might be lawsuits or disputes that were buried or hushed up that could point us to someone with a grudge. Like her ex."

As I'm about to pass by the table, Moxley barks. My

movements falter. A shiver scuttles down my spine. "Logan," I say, my voice barely above a whisper. "Look."

He's halfway into the living room and turns. "What is it?"

I point, and he returns to my side.

On the table is one of my canisters. Beside it lies a message, spelled out meticulously with dried black-eyed peas. The peas form words, each one a warning that chills me to the bone.

Let the dead rest, or you'll be next.

Chapter Fifteen

The black-eyed peas stare back at us, arranged in a messy block of letters, a faint, earthy scent lingering in the space. A Southern cooking staple turned sinister.

Mama would be horrified—not just at the message, but at the waste of perfectly good peas that could've been part of a New Year's Hoppin' John.

Because the threat is made with legumes, though, it's hard to take it seriously.

At least for me.

For Logan, not so much. "What in the devil...?" He scans the kitchen for other disturbances. "Did Birdie do this?"

That's my guess. "Why would she be upset if I'm looking into Donna's death? Or does she mean her own?" I touch one of the beans. "And if it's not her, we have a real problem."

Which seems weird. A ghost leaving threatening messages should be worse, right?

"I may have an odd sense of humor after years of dealing with criminal elements," my husband says, "but even I draw the line at death threats via beans." He places a protective hand on my shoulder. "Don't touch anything."

I back away from the table, bumping into Moxley, who lets out a concerned whine. The Bassett hound paws my foot, his long ears brushing the tile floor, as even he seems to sense the wrongness in our kitchen.

I pet him and remember his bark when we were outside. The shadow I saw. Mox doesn't usually notice ghosts, and the shadow seemed more solid and less ghostly, now that I think about it.

Logan gestures for me to follow him. "Let's check the security cameras, just to be sure."

His long strides eat up the way to my office as I half-jog beside him, mentally cataloging who, besides Birdie, might have a reason to threaten us. The list is uncomfortably long. Someone connected to Donna, like her killer or an overzealous fan? Someone like...Justin?

Or could it be someone connected to Birdie who fears the truth about her death will come to life?

Logan slides into the desk chair while I hover behind him, one hand on his shoulder, my fingers drumming on it. He navigates the security app, and I point at the screen as the footage from the front door camera loads. "Start it about half an hour ago, when we went out to chat with Brax and Rhys."

The video plays, showing our empty front porch for several minutes. Then, a figure appears—tall, slender, and built like a man. He's wearing a dark hoodie pulled low over his face.

"That's not a ghost," I whisper, though there's no need to be quiet. "Do we know him?"

Logan squints at the screen. "Can't tell with that hood. But look at how he moves—confident, like he knows we're out back."

I rub my arm. "We weren't exactly quiet out there. Anyone could have heard us."

He resumes the footage. The stranger tries the door, which we left unlocked, because this is Thornhollow. Even with the things that have happened to me, I forget sometimes to be more careful. "He just walked right in." Anger boils in my veins. My gaze flicks to the entryway as if I can see his form there. "Did he take anything?"

"The timestamp indicates that he was in here for exactly five minutes and twenty-seven seconds. Then he walked out, closing the door behind him. His hands are empty."

"He just came in to leave us a creepy message made out of black-eyed peas?" My stomach knots. The incident makes me feel vulnerable. Stupid. "Like, who does that?"

Logan's jaw tightens, a muscle twitching beneath his tanned skin. He replays the footage. "Look there," he says, pointing to the screen. "When he enters, you can see something in his right hand. Something small."

It's not like he's still present, but the idea of a stranger strolling into my house makes my skin crawl. The knot in my belly tightens. I lean closer, our heads nearly touching as we both stare at the frozen image of the stranger. "A phone? A weapon?"

"Can't tell," Logan admits, frustration creeping into his voice. "But whatever it is, he wasn't carrying it when he left."

The realization hits us both at the same time. We glance around. "He left something."

Logan stands, the chair rolling backward with the

sudden movement. "We need to search the house. Every corner. Whatever he left, we need to find it."

"But why?" I follow him, trying to ignore the voice in my head that sounds suspiciously like Aunt Willa. *Sometimes trouble comes looking for you, no matter how many sugar cookies you bake or how politely you greet your neighbors.* "Maybe whatever he was carrying, he stuck it in his pocket before he left. Like I said, it was probably his phone."

After our initial search turns up nothing out of the ordinary, Logan looks like he's ready to kill someone. "I'm calling Jones."

"Wait." I catch his wrist. "Think about this. What exactly do we tell him? That someone arranged legumes into a threat while we were chatting in the backyard?"

"That someone broke into our home, Ava."

I sigh, knowing he's right but also feeling the familiar weight of Jones's skepticism. "Jones already thinks I'm the town kook who talks to thin air. If we call him without solid evidence, he'll only brush it aside."

"We have the security footage. And I don't give a flying fig what Jones thinks about your abilities. This is about keeping you safe."

My phone buzzes on the desk, saving me from having to respond. It's a text from Sage.

There's a man in a dark sedan parked at the tea shop. Not sure if friend or foe, but definitely giving off major creeper vibes.

My stomach drops faster than a cast-iron skillet knocked off the stove.

"What?" Logan asks, noticing my expression.

I wordlessly hand him the phone. His eyes narrow as he

reads the message, and I can practically see the protective instinct radiating off him like heat waves.

He hands it back, and I call Sage. She answers on the first ring. "What does he look like?" I ask, putting her on speakerphone.

"Can you get a license plate?" Logan demands.

"Can't see a plate from here without being obvious," she says. "And he's difficult to describe because he's facing away from me. Do you want me to confront him?"

"No," we chorus. Logan leans on the desk. "He could be dangerous."

"He keeps adjusting something on his dashboard. I think it's a camera or maybe a phone? Is he filming your house?" Sounds of her shifting can be heard through the phone. "Um...I think he's white with dark hair. My angle is all wrong, though, and there isn't enough light."

"First the break-in and the threat, now surveillance?" Logan looks apocalyptic. "Ava, this is escalating. I'm going over there to confront him."

"He threatened you?" Sage asks.

I give her the rundown while holding onto Logan's arm. "There's a message written in black-eyed peas on the kitchen table, suggesting I stop investigating the dead or I'll end up in the same predicament. At first, I thought it was Birdie's ghost, but now I think it's him. Whoever *he* is."

"Wait," she says. "I think he just got a call. Should I hex his phone so the camera stops working? Nothing permanent, just enough to fog the lens?"

Despite everything, a smile tugs at my lips. Sage's offering of magical interference is so quintessentially her—

practical, protective, and just a touch mischievous. It's comforting in its own way.

"We're beyond that," Logan replies, clearly working through scenarios. "It's probably some stupid paparazzi trying to get a story about Donna's death, but it doesn't make sense for him to break in here. Unless…"

"What?" I ask.

In the distance, we hear a siren. Logan and I share a look. His eyes hold a smidge of panic, which is exactly what's blooming in my stomach. "Did you call the police?" I ask Sage.

"No, but it sounds like they're coming. Did you?"

"Not yet." I tap the desktop with my fingernail. "Who else would call them?"

Logan shakes his head. "A neighbor who saw the break-in? But our neighbors are Brax, Rhys, and Sage."

My hospitality has its limits, most especially when someone's using my pantry staples to threaten my life. "Well, if our visitor wants to scare me off, he's accomplished the opposite." I cross my arms, feeling that familiar stubbornness rise up—the same trait Daddy says I inherited from my great-grandmother. "We need to do another search. I suspect he left us a *gift* and then called the police to come find it."

Logan's face goes ashen. "He planted evidence."

"For what?" Sage asks with urgency. "Do you want me to come and help?"

"Thanks, but you keep an eye on our intruder," I tell her. "We'll handle things here."

"Let's split up." Logan heads for the living room. "You take your office and the kitchen, I'll search the main living area and my office."

Trepidation makes my pulse race like a horse in the Kentucky Derby. I check shelves and drawers, the nearing siren making my mouth dry. "If I were a nefarious villain," I mutter, racing to Rosie's office and rummaging through her drawers, "where would I hide incriminating evidence?"

"Somewhere obvious but overlooked," comes a lilting voice from behind me. "Like hiding a diamond in a bowl of cubic zirconia."

I nearly jam my finger in a drawer as I spin around. My guardian angel materializes in a flowing paisley mini-dress with bell sleeves that would make Twiggy jealous. Her red hair is teased into a perfect coif, and enormous blue hoop earrings dangle nearly to her shoulders. "Persephone! Don't sneak up on me like that!"

She laughs. "If you could see your face right now. Besides, I didn't sneak. I materialized. Completely different."

Logan shoots out of his office, eyes wide. "What?"

He can't see her. I point in her direction. "Persephone finally showed up. Any luck?"

He shakes his head and ducks back into the room. "Can't she just tell us where and what it is?"

"Men," Persephone sighs dramatically. "Always looking but never seeing. Sherlock's the same way." She clasps her hands. "You know I can't tell you who did it or why, but I'm excellent at scavenger hunts. Had lots of practice at Woodstock. Though we were usually hunting for, well... never mind."

"This is serious, Persephone. Someone is threatening me."

She floats a few inches off the floor. "Help is what

guardian angels do, you know. That and critiquing your wardrobe choices."

I resume searching, checking under Rosie's desk. The only thing there is Fern's bed. "Can't you just...I don't know...sense where it is?"

"Darling, I'm not a bloodhound."

She begins to hum a tune that sounds suspiciously like *These Boots Are Made for Walkin* as she heads for the kitchen.

I rush after her. The siren is almost here. "You're getting colder than a January skinny-dip," she announces as I search through cabinets.

I pause. "Are you playing hot and cold with me?"

She winks. "You're freezing."

I move toward the refrigerator. "How about now?"

"Still cold as Donna Dean's heart."

Logan gives me a curious glance as he checks the garbage can. "Nothing. Let me check the entryway."

"Cold!" Persephone sings out.

"Not there," I tell him. "Where?" I ask her.

Persephone floats into the room and stares at the pantry.

I lay a hand on the door.

"Getting hotter," she says.

I fling it open.

"Hot tamale!" Persephone fans herself dramatically.

I shuffle through the cans, bags, and boxes. I don't see anything out of the ordinary. I crouch low. That's where I would hide something. "Here?"

Persephone does a little shimmy in midair. "You're on fire, now!"

I run my hands between a bag of potatoes and my Crock Pot.

"What are you doing?" Logan asks. "Is Persephone telling you it's there?"

"Sort of," I reply.

Then I notice the small gap between the wall and the flooring at the very rear of the pantry.

"Bingo!" Persephone squeals. "If this were the Dating Game, you'd have just won a trip to the Bahamas!"

Wedged at the back is a small plastic bag.

The police car's siren is so loud, I have to raise my voice, "Logan! Look!"

He's beside me in an instant, shining a flashlight on it. "Be careful of your fingerprints." He tugs out a clean hand-kerchief from his pocket and hands it to me.

I use it to remove the bag. It's light. "What do we do now?"

Persephone floats out of the kitchen. I chase after her. The siren cuts off, but blue lights flash through the front display windows.

Arthur raises his head to peer out. Seemingly uncon-cerned, he stands up, curls around three times, and goes back to sleep.

A car door slams.

"That's right." Persephone nods approvingly. "I'm really good at my job."

I'm too anxious to roll my eyes. Logan takes the bag, holding it up. "Let's see what our uninvited guest left us."

My heart pounds as Logan carefully opens it. Perse-phone hovers just over his shoulder, peering down with undisguised curiosity.

"Oh my," she whispers, her playful demeanor suddenly subdued. "That doesn't look like a housewarming gift."

A loud knock comes from the door.

"Don't answer that. Not yet." Logan tips the bag onto the top of my desk. What spills out makes my stomach drop—a handful of small, withered mushrooms, their caps bruised and ominous.

My dry throat makes my voice come out screechy. "Is that what I think it is?"

"Destroying Angel mushrooms," my guardian angel says.

My hands tremble as I connect the dots. "Logan, these are the same kind of mushrooms that killed Donna."

His face hardens. "Whoever is across the street is trying to frame you."

The doorbell peals with successive rings. Whoever is here is getting impatient. Pretty sure I know who it is.

"Why me?" I reach for my phone. Sage is still on the line. "Got to call you back."

"Should I come over? Why is Detective Jones here?" she asks.

"Because whoever broke into my house wants me to take the fall for what they did." I disconnect and hit the speed button for Daddy.

"We need a plan." Logan's hands grip the edge of the desk, knuckles white. "Now. We've got the security footage showing the intruder. That's evidence in our favor."

"But if Jones finds these mushrooms here..." I gesture to the deadly fungi.

"We'll handle this carefully." His eyes, usually so calm and measured, are intense. "We're going to show Jones the footage, hand over the mushrooms, and explain exactly what happened. We have nothing to hide."

"Except a guardian angel who helped us find the evidence," I mutter.

"I'd leave that part out if I were you," Persephone suggests helpfully from her perch in my office chair. "Detective Jones already thinks you're loony."

A pounding starts up on the front door. Logan hesitates, quickly kissing my forehead. "I don't want this guy to get away. I'll slip out the back and grab Brax. We'll catch him, and Jones can get a confession out of him."

The doorbell sets off again, its cheerful chime now a warning bell.

My father picks up as I watch Logan tear out of the room. "Hey, Daddy."

"Everything alright, sweetheart?"

"Not exactly." I glance at the bag of mushrooms while Persephone hovers, making exaggerated eavesdropping gestures. "Someone broke into our house while Logan and I were in the backyard. They left a threatening message spelled out in black-eyed peas and planted a bag of toxic mushrooms like the ones that killed Donna Dean in my pantry. The intruder is across the street, filming our house from Sage's parking lot, and Jones is beating down the front door. I suspect the man framing me called him."

Dad whistles softly under his breath. "Did your cameras catch the intruder?"

"Yes, we caught the whole thing on video. Tall guy in a hoodie. Came through the front door bold as brass."

"Good girl." Despite everything, I feel a flush of pride. "And the mushrooms—you're sure they're the same kind?"

"Pretty sure. Some divine guidance assures me they are."

"Ava Fantome," Jones yells through the door. "Open up."

"Daddy, what do I do?"

"Avalon," my father says, using my full name the way he always does when he needs my full attention, "Landon Jones is a good detective. Show him the footage first thing. Don't wait for him to ask. Hand over those mushrooms. Tell him everything exactly as it happened."

"Everything?" I ask, glancing at Persephone, who's now pretending to be Detective Jones, puffing out her cheeks and furrowing her brow in a comical impression.

"Well," Dad chuckles, "maybe not the parts involving your spectral friends."

I take a deep breath. "Okay. Show the footage, hand over the mushrooms, tell the truth."

"And Ava? Remember you've done nothing wrong. I'll be there in a few minutes."

His words wrap around me like a protective shield. "Thanks, Daddy." I disconnect. "Time to face the music."

"Break a leg!" Persephone calls after me, then reconsiders. "Well, not literally. That would be inconvenient."

Show the footage. Hand over the mushrooms. Tell the truth.

I can do this.

Moxley waddles along with me as I go to answer the door, his jowls quivering.

The door beating continues. I take a breath so deep my lungs might touch my spine, plaster on what Mama calls a 'company smile,' and pull open the door.

Jones fills the doorframe like a thundercloud in a police

uniform. His brows are drawn together, creating a single dark line above eyes. He doesn't bother with pleasantries— never has, not even when Dad was his boss. His voice is as flat and unyielding as a parking lot. "I hear you're a killer."

Chapter Sixteen

"Detective Jones." I channel every ounce of Southern courtesy Mama has drilled into me over the years. "I was just about to call you. Please, come in." I gesture toward my office. "I have something you need to see."

His eyes narrow a fraction, skepticism radiating off him. He steps inside, his gaze immediately sweeping the room with meticulous professionalism. "Gotta call about you being involved with—"

"Before you say anything else, I need to tell you that someone broke into our house tonight."

His expression doesn't change. "And you didn't report it?"

"It just happened. I have security footage."

I bring him to my desk and step aside so he can see before I hit play. As the hooded figure enters the front door, I watch Jones's face instead of the screen. His expression remains impassive, but I've known him since I was a child— that slight tightening around his mouth speaks volumes.

"And there's this," I continue, pointing at the bag of mushrooms. "He left these hidden in the pantry. I believe he's also responsible for a threatening message left on my kitchen table."

Persephone floats by and makes a face. "Yeah, about that... That wasn't your intruder." I give her a questioning look. I don't want to say anything in front of the detective, but she gets the point and shrugs. "You were right that Birdie left that message."

And she didn't tell me this until *now?*

Jones uses a pencil to move the bag around, examining the contents. "These look like—"

"Destroying Angel mushrooms," I finish. "The same kind that killed Donna."

The air between us crackles with tension. I can practically hear the gears turning in his head, recalculating whatever theory brought him to my door.

"Someone's trying to frame me." I hesitate. I'm confused why Birdie would leave such a message. Could Persephone be wrong? "Someone spelled out a threat with black-eyed peas on my kitchen table."

Jones's eyebrows inch up slightly—the closest thing to surprise I've ever seen on his face. He asks to see it, and the surprise deepens to concern. "Who would go through all this trouble to frame you?"

I long for a cup of tea to calm my nerves. "I didn't know Donna until she showed up at The Honey Bee. I have no motive, and plenty of others do, but I guess I'm an easy scapegoat for the killer."

"Where's your husband?"

"Across the street. Someone is in Sage's parking lot

filming the front of the house. I'll give you three guesses who it might be."

He heads for the door. "Looks like we'd best go have a talk with him."

I fly out of the house on his heels, but before we cross the street, I pull up short. There's no car in the parking lot, and my husband and Brax are talking to Sage on the quaint front porch of her shop.

When they see us, Logan's shoulders fall, and he shakes his head. As Jones and I join them, Logan says, "He got away."

"Did you get his plates?" Jones asks.

Another head shake. "The car didn't have any."

Persephone has trailed after us. She takes a seat at one of the outdoor bistro tables, picking at her nails. "Birdie left a message for the intruder, not you."

Ah. That makes a bit more sense. Birdie was...defending me?

Jones pulls out his trusty notepad. He makes us start at the beginning and go through everything we said and did since arriving home. Brax confirms that we were outback talking to him and Rhys when the break-in occurred, and Sage has pictures of the vehicle that she snapped through her windows.

Jones recovers the mushrooms and tells Logan to send him a copy of the security camera footage. He assures us he'll put out a BOLO for the car.

Daddy arrives with Mama shortly after Jones leaves, and Logan and I have to tell the story again.

Daddy hugs me and assures me he'll help Jones locate the man. Mama paces the floor, torn between being sympathetic and supportive and freaking out about the cookoff and what this will mean for it.

We open a bottle of wine, but my stomach is too tangled in knots to enjoy it.

My teenage intern, Lia, texts me: *What did you do? The blog is getting all kinds of hate comments. So are the socials. They're claiming you killed Donna Dean!*

I rub my forehead, a splitting headache now present. I assure her I had nothing to do with it and ask her to shut down commenting on all of our feeds until this is cleared up.

She tells me she's already on it. While her obsession with ghost-hunting is often concerning, I'm fortunate to have her for marketing and keeping our accounting in order.

When Mama hears about the hate comments, she goes into mayoral mode. She knows how to spin cotton into a silk purse. "First thing in the morning, we hold a press conference and bring to light this horrible person's pathetic attempt at disparaging your reputation. We'll have this cleared up by noon, you mark my words."

She's skilled at this sort of thing, having successfully handled many political opponents who tried to tarnish her reputation. However, it's not my style to hold a press conference to defend myself, but I need to put myself in her hands. She tells me to keep my chin up, and Daddy gives me a big hug again before they leave.

As expected, I don't sleep. Neither does Logan. He mostly stays in his office, coming out on occasion to check on me, and he leaves early the following morning after taking Moxley for a walk. When Rosie shows up, I'm wrung out and overly emotional. She's heard the gossip, and she brings me a tall coffee and pastry from The Honey Bar. "What are you going to do?"

"Hold a press conference, I guess. It's what Mama told me to do."

"Are you nervous? Do you think people will listen?"

"I honestly have no idea. Seems like people don't want the truth anymore; they just want drama."

When I arrive at City Hall at the appointed time, Mama is there, and someone I don't expect—Detective Jones.

I'm relieved, surprised, and wary. What's he up to?

Mama hands me a handwritten speech in her perfect script and gives me a list of orders to follow. She ends with a lift of her chin. "You've got this."

The windows of City Hall reflect the mid-morning light. Logan stands off to the side and blows me an air kiss as Mama steps to the podium. I worry the paper in my nervous hands, noting many familiar faces in the crowd. I do as Mama says, keeping my face serene as panic blooms in my stomach. I'm the picture of innocence regardless of my fear.

As I scan the crowd, I wonder if last night's intruder is here. *Is he Donna's killer? Is this what he wants?* To turn the attention and spotlight off himself and onto me?

"...and I can assure you all that our town's safety remains the top priority," Mama declares, her voice carrying across the town square. She's got her Sunday best on—a pale blue dress with pearl buttons that catch the Georgia sunlight—but her knuckles are white around the edges of the podium.

I shift from one foot to the other, feeling the tension rising in the crowd. Mrs. Abernathy fans herself with a church bulletin while old Mr. Flannery keeps clearing his throat like he's about to speak up, but never does.

"Is it true there's a killer among us?" someone calls from the back.

I wince and catch snippets of whispered conversations around me: "...never would've happened if Nash was chief..." and "...that girl was always trouble..." The latter is accompanied by not-so-subtle glances in my direction.

Mama taps the microphone. "Now, now. Let's maintain our Southern dignity. Detective Jones has graciously agreed to update us on the investigation."

Jones steps forward, and the onlookers tense. His dark uniform is freshly pressed, despite the humidity, and his expression remains as unyielding as ever, revealing absolutely nothing.

Mama catches his eye, and he gives her a single, deliberate nod. She relinquishes the microphone and stands next to me.

"Morning, folks." Jones's deep voice instantly quiets the murmurs. "I appreciate your patience during this difficult time."

He hasn't looked at me once, which could be a good thing or a very bad thing. He adjusts the microphone, the feedback whining briefly before he continues, his voice a stark contrast to the earlier chaos. "I know y'all have questions, and I'm here to provide answers." The square is so quiet you could hear a peach pit drop. "The investigation into Donna Dean's death has taken a significant turn."

Around me, the crowd buzzes. Over to the left, a lady whispers something to her friend, which makes the woman's eyes widen. To my right, Mama nods sagely as if she's known all along whatever Jones is about to say. When I glance at my husband, Logan winks at me.

"We have new evidence that exonerates—" Jones begins, but his words are cut short by a commotion on the street.

The car from last night screeches to a stop, creating a dust cloud, and Justin Bowles exits, leaving the driver's door open. His phone is in his hand and he holds it high. "That's right, folks! Live from Thornhollow, where justice is about to be served!"

The crowd parts like the Red Sea as he strides forward. His eyes are bloodshot, his hair disheveled, but he's smiling like he's just won the lottery. "Detective, why don't you tell my viewers the truth?" he calls out, his voice pitched for maximum drama. "Tell them you know who killed my fiancée!"

Jones remains impassive, though my jaw drops. *Fiancée?* Everyone knows they broke up ages ago. He's milking this for everything he can, giving his viewers a live feed they must be soaking up.

Jones raises a hand. "Mr. Bowles, this is not the appropriate time for your theatrics."

"It's her!" Justin stabs a finger in my direction, and every eye sweeps to me. "Ava Fantome-Cross killed Donna! She was jealous that Donna was going to be the top judge, and she murdered her in cold blood!"

The crowd gasps. Mrs. Collins clutches her pearls so hard I worry she'll snap the string. Her husband, who usually can't hear a tornado siren, somehow hears every word and is now pointing his cane at me. "Did you do it?"

"She hated Donna!" Justin uses his phone to pan between my face and the crowd. "Everyone knows it! Tell them, Detective! Tell them what she did!"

My stomach feels like it's full of uncooked grits. I've been accused of many things in Thornhollow—being strange, talking to myself (which, fair enough, but the ghosts don't know I'm the only one who can hear them), even putting too much sugar in the church lemonade—but never murder.

"I most certainly did not," I say, but my voice is drowned out by a dozen folks talking and calling for explanations.

Mama straightens. "Now you listen here, Mr. Bowles—" she starts, but Jones holds up a hand, silencing her with a look that even Mama respects.

The crowd is a sea of shocked faces and frantically texting fingers. Reporters are surging closer to the podium with handheld recorders and microphones.

I meet Logan's calm expression, then glance at Daddy in the back of the crowd in sunglasses and a cap. To his left is Kit. To his right, Sage. A few rows in front of them are faces from yesterday—Missy, Bo, Raylene, and Shane.

They all seem shocked, except maybe Bo. He's nodding, as if Justin has won him over.

Detective Jones regards Justin with clinical detachment mixed with barely concealed distaste. His voice booms over the crowd. "Mr. Bowles, since you're so eager to share your thoughts, why don't you join me up here?"

My heart stutters. Is Jones actually giving this man a platform? A bigger one than he already has with his live streaming?

I feel sick. I shoot a panicked glance at Mama, but she only grasps my hand and gives it a squeeze.

Justin's face splits into a victorious grin as he pushes through the crowd, phone still recording. "Gladly." He bounds up the steps like he's accepting an award. The gathered townsfolk press closer, necks craning. The reporters lift their recorders higher, jostling each other to get prime space.

As Justin approaches, I catch a whiff of expensive cologne mixed with what I'm pretty sure is whiskey. He gives me a confident, wicked smile. Does Jones actually believe him? Is this some kind of terrible Georgia justice where the loudest accuser wins?

"Folks," Justin says, leaning into the microphone with ease, "what the police aren't telling you is that this woman"—he points at me—"has extreme mental issues. Ask anyone in town, and they'll tell you that she talks to the dead!"

Another of those collective gasps echoes through the space. I want to dissolve into a puddle. Plenty of folks know about my ghost-whispering, but others don't. Or didn't until now.

Jones steps between Justin and the microphone, effectively cutting him off. "Thank you for that completely erroneous statement," Jones says. "Now, let me share some facts with the good people gathered here." He glances at Justin's phone and yanks it from his hand. "And for all you watching this feed."

"Hey!" Justin lunges for it, but Jones shifts his substantial frame, blocking the man with practiced ease. Justin stumbles and nearly falls.

Jones grabs him by the back of his shirt and plants him next to the podium. "Fact number one." He removes a folded document from his breast pocket. "On March seventeenth of this year, Donna Dean filed for and was granted a restraining order against her ex-boyfriend, one Justin Bowles." He releases his hold on Justing and unfolds the paper with deliberate slowness. "The order specifically prohibited Mr.

Bowles from approaching within five hundred feet of her residence or place of business."

The crowd sucks in a collective breath. "That's—that's taken out of context!" Justin sputters, his confident demeanor cracking. "It was a misunderstanding, that's all."

Many in the crowd trade glances. Voices rise and fall.

"Fact number two," Jones continues as if Justin hasn't spoken. "Mr. Bowles was observed by multiple witnesses approaching Ms. Dean at The Peach Pit diner three weeks ago over in Somerville, resulting in an altercation that required intervention by the staff."

Justin's face flushes an alarming shade of gray-white. "That was—I was just trying to talk to her! We were working things out!" His voice climbs. "Donna would tell you herself if she... if she were here!"

"Is that why she had to be escorted to her car by the busboy?" Logan asks, stepping forward. "Because you were 'working things out'?"

"You." Justin points an accusatory finger at my husband. "Of course, you're here to defend her. You're her lawyer husband, who gets her off the hook all the time."

Jones continues without missing a beat, raising his voice. "Fact number three. The night before Ms. Dean's death, Mr. Bowles checked into the Nottingham Hotel under a *false name*. Someone working at the hotel recognized him."

Raylene flicks a glance to Shane, and the two of them begin threading their way out of the crowd toward the sidewalk.

"I have business interests here!" Justin's voice cracks. "This is—this is character assassination! You've got nothing connecting me to Donna's death!"

And he hasn't assassinated my character? Yeesh.

The crowd's mood is shifting like the weather before a storm. The same town that was ready to believe the worst about me is now reassessing things, their eyes narrowing as they look at Justin. Another wave of relief tinged with anxiety rushes through me.

"I loved Donna!" Justin insists, grabbing for the microphone. "I would never hurt her! This is all circumstantial, and you know it!"

Jones doesn't even flinch as he blocks Justin's reach. "Circumstantial, like the threatening comments you left on Ms. Dean's blog over the past year? Circumstantial, like the character assassinations you did on *her* in your culinary videos?" He glances at his notepad, which he's pulled from his front pocket. "Let's see what you said in your last one. *Donna is a terrible cook and a worthless human being.*"

The crowd gasps. Jones glares at him. "That is what you said, isn't it? Season three, episode five. I watched a mess of them last night, and I can tell you, son, she had every right to bring more than a restraining order against you. Slander is unlawful, and she should've taken you to court."

Justin's face contorts. "Those weren't—I never—you can't prove—"

I watch him unravel before my eyes. He's now a desperate, flailing man, realizing his carefully constructed lies are collapsing. "*She loved me.*" His voice drops to a hoarse whisper. "Everything I did was because I loved her."

Jones closes his notepad. "Mr. Bowles, in my experience, love doesn't typically involve restraining orders."

Chapter Seventeen

But the show isn't over.

Detective Jones motions at Logan. My husband steps forward, carrying a folder, which he sets on the podium and opens.

"What I have here," he says, tapping the folder, "are police reports from Atlanta PD dating back three years. Reports that somehow never made it into the system." He pauses, upping the drama, and I wonder if he's been around Mama too long. "These are reports of domestic disturbances at Ms. Dean's residence. Six separate incidents where neighbors called in concerns. Every one of them involved the man standing here, Justin Bowles."

A murmur ripples through the crowd. Beside me, Mama's hand squeezes mine again.

More people begin to filter out. One of them is Bo Remington. He shakes his head. Shane and Raylene are nowhere to be found. My gut tells me there's something suspicious about it.

"That's a lie!" Justin's face flushes crimson. "Those were —we were just having loud discussions! Creative differences! We are both hot-blooded people. Passionate about our food and culinary preferences." He snatches up his phone, jabbing at the screen frantically before shoving it in his pocket.

Apparently, the live stream is over.

"Creative differences that resulted in broken furniture? A dislocated shoulder that Ms. Dean claimed was from *falling down stairs*?" Logan's voice remains even, but there's steel beneath the calm. "The officer who took that report noted suspicious bruising patterns inconsistent with a fall."

The townsfolk's voices now rise in a tide of judgment. Justin holds out his hands, appealing to them. "She was everything to me! I would never hurt her—never! She was my meal ticket—I mean, my *muse*!"

Justin's slip makes my stomach churn. I scan the crowd, noting how differently they're looking at him now.

"He's drowning," I murmur to Mama.

"Good," she says with no small amount of exuberance. "Let him."

I should feel vindicated, watching him get his comeup-pance. The man tried to frame me for murder, after all. But there's something unsettling about watching someone's life collapse in public, even when they deserve it. It's like watching a car crash in slow motion—horrible, but you can't look away.

"Those reports are fabricated." He's become a trapped animal, snarling now. "Donna would tell you herself if she were here!"

"That's just it, Mr. Bowles." Logan closes the folder with

a snap. "She's not here to tell us anything. And you had the most to gain from making sure of that."

Sadness over Donna's death hits me. A sucker punch. I didn't even know her. She doesn't sound like a nice person. But it's still there.

Logan shifts aside so Jones can resume his stand at the microphone. The detective reaches into his pocket and pulls out a USB drive. "What we have here," he says, turning the device in his thick fingers, "is security footage recovered from Mr. and Mrs. Cross's home surveillance system." He glances at me with the barest acknowledgment before continuing. "Time-stamped footage shows Mr. Bowles entering their property at ten thirty-three last night."

The crowd inhales so dramatically, it would be comical if my skin wasn't crawling at the memory of it.

"That's a lie!" Justin tries to grab the USB. Jones knocks his hand away. "I've never been to their—"

Bo hurriedly slips past those nearest him and heads off down the sidewalk. Sage and Kit watch him go, then turn their attention back to us. Meanwhile, Daddy threads his way out of the crowd and follows.

"We have you on camera, Mr. Bowles." Jones's voice is level but firm. "Entering through the front door, leaving a threatening note on the kitchen counter, and planting evidence to frame Ava."

Justin's face goes slack. It drains of all color. "What?" He glances at me, seeming bewildered. "I didn't... That's not true."

Logan leans close. "I told you those cameras were worth having."

They have come in handy a time or two, even though I

hate spying on folks. "Remind me to never complain about them again."

The murmurs in the crowd morph into open hostility toward Justin now. Jones raises his hand for silence, and the crowd obeys. "Furthermore," he announces, reaching for paperwork on the podium's hidden shelf, "Judge Carmichael has issued search warrants for Mr. Bowles's hotel room, his rental car, and all personal belongings."

Justin reels, desperation etched across his face. "You can't do that! I have rights! I have—"

"Officers have already begun the search," Jones continues, completely unfazed. "Preliminary findings include a burner phone with threatening text messages sent to the victim and a set of her house keys that she reported missing last month."

The same people who were giving me side-eye now look at me with something that might almost be respect—or at least the decency to appear embarrassed about their previous assumptions.

"I don't understand," I whisper to Logan. "How did you and Jones put this together so quickly?"

Logan's face is grim but satisfied. "He may not like you much, Ava, but the man's a good detective. Your Dad and I just filled in a few pieces for him."

A flash of iridescent fabric catches my eye. I spot Persephone hovering near the path my father took, the bell sleeves of her bright yellow dress fluttering. She waves before disappearing in the same direction.

"But Justin *is* our culprit, right?"

He puts his lips close to my ear. "The truth is, we don't have a clear shot of Justin's face on the camera footage, nor do we have his fingerprints on the door handle. Baldwin reported that he was in the bar last night with friends at the time of our break-in."

My stomach drops. "Why didn't you tell me? If he was at the hotel, then... Who's trying to frame me?"

"That's what we're going to figure out. Anyone could have taken Justin's car, and without a clear photo of him driving it, or entering our house? Any good attorney could punch holes in our theory that it was him."

Two uniformed officers approach Justin, one holding handcuffs. The crowd hushes, collectively holding its breath as Detective Jones gestures toward the squad car parked at the curb. "Justin Bowles, you're under arrest for harassment, breaking and entering, and as a person of interest in the death of Donna Dean."

Justin's shoulders stiffen. "This is ridiculous! You're making a mistake. I'm being set up!"

"You have the right to remain silent," the officer begins, securing the cuffs around Justin's wrists.

I should feel vindicated, but instead, there's only a hollow fear where my anger was.

Justin Bowles isn't the killer.

Or is he?

Just because he isn't the one who planted evidence in my house and made false accusations against me, doesn't mean he didn't murder Donna.

Justin twists in the officers' grip as they guide him toward the waiting vehicle. His eyes lock onto mine across the square—dark, glittering with a hatred so pure it makes me take an involuntary step back.

"This isn't over," he yells, his voice dripping with venom.

"You think you've won? You haven't seen anything yet. My fans will destroy you!"

Logan steps protectively in front of me, but I move beside him, refusing to cower. "I'm not afraid of you," I call back, surprising myself with my steady voice. "And I *will* get justice for Donna."

Mama rushes to the microphone, plastering on her mayoral smile. "Now, don't y'all forget, the Southern Spirits Cookoff kicks off tonight at five at the fairgrounds three miles north of town. Those with tickets get to taste-test and vote for their favorites in the categories of Apparitions & Appetizers and The Spirits' Sides. From ten to noon tomorrow will be our Main Courses from the Morgue, and from noon to three will be the Death By Desserts category. As a bonus, we've also added a Conjured Cocktails & Haunted Sips happy hour. The winners in each category will be announced at the end of the evening. And be sure to check out the silent auction. All proceeds will benefit the Birdie Birmingham Charity!"

As the crowd begins to disperse, some of the reporters ask me for a comment. I brush them off, wadding up Mama's unused speech.

Persephone materializes next to me. "Well, that was more exciting than the time I crashed Janis Joplin's private party."

"Please don't," I groan, turning away from the view of the reporters and those still lingering. "And where have you been?" Logan gives me a raised brow. I have to explain. "My guardian angel has made another appearance."

He nods. Mama motions for us to follow her inside to her office, but Persephone signals me to follow her to one of the town hall pillars. I tell my mother and Logan that I'll be right there.

"While everyone was watching the detective's show, I was watching the watchers." Persephone taps her temple with a fluorescent pink fingernail. "Raylene, Shane, and Bo? They looked scared, not guilty. Your daddy thought so, too. That's why he kept an eye on them."

"And? Did he catch them doing something suspicious?"

"No, but don't give up hope."

Hope is at war with the rest of my emotions. Across the square, Sage is talking with her boyfriend, Bisby, and Kit. The three of them huddle together. When they catch my eye, Sage urgently waves me over.

I make my way toward my friends, overhearing snippets of conversation from the dispersing crowd.

"...always knew that Bowles fella was no good..."

"...Fantome girl sure attracts trouble..."

Kit pulls me into a quick hug when I reach them. "You okay? That was intense."

"I'm fine," I say, though my mind is racing. "What gives?"

Bisby shifts uncomfortably, his tall frame somehow trying to make itself smaller. "Hate to bother you, but I've been hearing things. Whispers. Not from the living."

Bis hears ghosts, and sometimes sees them like I do. A familiar prickle of unease scratches at the back of my neck. "Whispers about what?"

"About Birdie," Sage interjects. "And Lorna."

Tabitha crosses the lawn in her human form, hailing me. At least she's dressed. "Aye. I've heard the whispers, too," she says, her Scottish accent dancing over the words.

My unease grows. "What are they saying?"

She stares off toward the north. "There is more to what happened to Birdie than anyone's letting on."

Cryptic and not helpful. "What are the ghosts saying?" I ask Bis.

"That plenty of folks back then suspected foul play with her disappearance, but no one was brave enough to do anything about it. Her stepfather silenced them."

"Stepfather? Steven Duval?"

Tabitha nods. "Too many questions and those with the answers have passed on, but the past never stays buried in Thornhollow."

Another avenue to investigate. A mystery to untangle. I glance around at the nearly empty square, the late morning sun bright on the spring grass, now trampled from too many feet.

"I've got to go talk to Mama," I tell them. "Let's meet at my house for lunch. It's time we figure out the truth about who killed Donna *and* Birdie."

As we disperse, I catch a glimpse of something by the old oak tree at the edge of the square. Just for a second, I swear I see a woman in a floral apron, her hair styled in soft 1960s waves, watching us with knowing eyes.

Birdie.

Then she's gone, like morning mist burning off in the Georgia sun.

Chapter Eighteen

I step into Mama's office, the door protesting my entrance with a loud creak. Mama looks pleased but still tense. Her fingers hover over files, pens, and her planner. Logan lounges in a guest chair, an ankle kicked over his opposite knee. "There you are." He stands and motions for me to sit in the matching chair.

"Ava, honey," Mama says. "We were just discussing the press conference."

I sink into the cushion and rub my forehead. "Yes, let's talk about that. You guys sort of blindsided me."

Logan's eyes meet mine. "I know and I'm sorry for that, but it was all thrown together so quickly, we didn't have time to do more than gather our plan of attack and go for it." He squeezes my hand. "We'll get through this, Ava. Nobody who knows you believes that man's accusations."

I'm grateful for his confidence. "How did you get all that dirt on him?"

He grins. "I have friends everywhere. Most of whom owe me favors."

I lean over and kiss him. "I sure appreciate it. What Jones did, too."

"Your father helped with that," Mama says. "He and Landon were up all night, hunting down those suppressed reports and waking the judge up for the search warrants."

"I owe them both." I squirm, searching for a way to phrase my next announcement. "Speaking of judges...I've been thinking." I twist my hands together. "Maybe I should step down from the contest. Raylene Stokes would be a much better fit. She's got the background and experience that I don't."

And she might have more insight into Justin if I can drag it out of her.

Mama's eyebrows shoot up. "Don't you dare go getting cold feet on me."

My resolve wavers. "But, with everything that's happened... I don't want to bring more negative attention to the contest. It's supposed to be about community and raising funds for Birdie's charity, not...murder accusations."

Logan shakes his head. "You can't let crazy rumors dictate your life."

While I agree with the sentiment, I'm still feeling unnerved. "There are too many people who may still believe I'm guilty. Or worse, what if I actually mess up the judging because I'm so stressed and don't have a clue what I'm doing?"

Mama's eyes narrow. "You listen here," she says, her voice carrying the weight of a thousand Sunday sermons. "You are not backing out of this contest. You have nothing to feel guilty or ashamed about, and you can't let Justin Bowles win. Is that what you want? To let his false charges browbeat you into hiding?"

"Well, no, but—"

She waves off my protest, reaching into her desk drawer and pulling out a crisp sheet of paper. She slides it across the polished oak surface. "This here is the judge's scorecard." She taps it with a perfectly manicured nail. "It's simpler than separating egg whites. You just rate each dish on taste, presentation, and creativity. Easy as pie—which, incidentally, you'll be judging too."

I reluctantly chuckle at her pun, even as my stomach does a nervous flip. "But Mama—"

"No buts." Her tone softens. "Honey, you've got more gumption in your little finger than most folks have in their whole body. This town needs you to stand strong, show 'em what you're made of. You told Justin Bowles that you weren't afraid of him. Time to put your money where your mouth is."

I glance at Logan. He's nodding along with Mama, a proud smile playing on his lips. "She's right. You can do this. You're Avalon Fantome-Cross. Owner of Enchanted Events. Wedding gown designer. President of the Chamber of Commerce." He uses a finger to lift my chin a notch. "And you're the mayor's daughter."

Mama beams. He knows how to schmooze with the best of them. "If it'll make you feel better," she says, "I can ask Raylene to fill Donna's spot."

Relief swamps me. Between Raylene, Bo, and Missy, I'll have plenty of help. And, plenty of people to interrogate more thoroughly. "I'd be happy to invite her, myself."

Mama nods. "If it eases your mind."

I go around the desk and hug her. "It does. Thank you."

Logan's phone buzzes. He glances at the screen, brow furrowing. "I need to take this."

He steps away, his voice low as he answers. When he turns back a moment later, his expression is a mix of apology and concern. "Sorry. Mr. Jameson is having a few issues with the contract we discussed yesterday. I need to swing by his office." He glances at me. "Any chance you can catch a ride home?"

I walk him to the door. "Don't worry about me. Go take care of your client."

He hesitates. "You're sure? With everything that's going on, maybe I should stay close."

"Go," I insist. I reach up and straighten his tie. "I'll text Sage or Kit. They might still be here."

Logan's expression softens. "Alright, but promise me you'll call if anything feels off. Even if it's just a hunch."

"Cross my heart." I draw an X over the area. "Go save Mr. Jameson from whatever legal tangle he's gotten himself into."

We share a quick kiss, and Logan leaves, his broad shoulders disappearing through the door. A pang of worry flutters in my chest, but I push it aside, shooting my friends a message. I'm a grown woman, for heaven's sake, not some damsel in distress.

As I turn back to Mama, thunder mutters in the distance. The air feels heavy, charged with electricity. I glance out the window to see dark clouds rolling in, their underbellies an ominous shade of green.

"Looks like we're in for a real frog-strangler," Mama says, following my gaze.

I pull out my phone and text Sage. "I need to get home. Rosie is handling this evening's wedding at the church, but I need to double-check that everything's set."

A gust of wind rattles the windows, carrying with it the scent of rain and ozone. The trees outside bend and sway. Mama checks her weather app. "Sure hope this blows out of here before the kickoff at five. The main building will keep the entrants dry, but a storm could keep folks from coming out."

Sage replies to my message—she's still here. "My ride is waiting," I tell her, giving her a quick kiss on the cheek. It smells of foundation and powder. "This is just a summer squall. It'll be gone before you know it."

As I step out into the hallway, another roll of thunder shakes the building. I quicken my pace, eager to meet Sage and not get drenched.

On the way home, the storm is more bark than bite. The windshield is barely wet, and we decide to stop at The Honey Bar.

I didn't expect Brax or Rhys to come to the press conference, since they both have businesses, but I missed seeing my best friend's face in the crowd. I want to check on him and get a fresh coffee.

The building's quaint facade is obscured by a sea of umbrellas and raincoats. I blink, hardly believing my eyes. The Honey Bar's lot is packed. A line snakes out the door and down the sidewalk, a colorful conga of rain-soaked patrons. "What the... Will you look at that crowd?"

Sage pulls up across the street, halfway down the block.

"Looks like half of Thornhollow's decided to weather the storm with a latte."

Through the front windows, I catch glimpses of a makeshift shrine forming on the counter with flickering candles, handwritten notes, and small mementos. Now it makes sense. "They're honoring Donna."

"Small town, big heart. And her fans have heard what a terrible time she had with Justin."

I fish my phone out of my purse. "Let me text Brax and see if he needs reinforcements."

There's no response. I try again, adding a string of coffee cup emojis for good measure.

We wait another minute.

Sage peers over at my screen. "Anything?"

"Radio silence. Poor guy must be drowning in orders."

She purses her lips. "I'd offer to help, but I have to get to my place to open up."

"I've got it." I send messages to Kit, Penn, and Jenn. The latter two are sisters. Jenn works part-time for me, and Penn has been there when I needed a helping hand.

We sit in contemplative silence, watching the steady stream of people braving the elements for caffeine and community. All three women respond, confirming they'll be at the coffee bar within the hour.

I share that with Sage, and she relaxes. "Guess we can go, then. I'll brew us some strong tea and share my latest muffins with you."

Fat droplets of rain splatter against the windshield. I squint through the growing moisture on the glass. "I'd appreciate it, but I do hate leaving Brax like this."

"He's probably reveling in the fact that he can do this for

Donna and her followers," Sage assures me. "I know he was worried that what happened could affect him and his business negatively. But this? This will bolster his confidence."

Just as Sage shifts the car into drive, a figure bursts out of The Honey Bar's door, shoving past the waiting crowd. It's Shane, tugging on a sweatshirt as he stumbles onto the sidewalk. His shoulders are hunched, his face a mask of what appears to be sadness. It's hard to tell through the intensifying downpour.

"What's he doing here?" I say. I glance back at the door, waiting for Raylene, but she doesn't follow.

Sage peers at his retreating figure. "He's not carrying any coffee or food, so it doesn't look like he stopped for breakfast. Why would he brave this crowd just to leave empty-handed?"

The reason isn't that obvious, but I'm sure of it. "For Donna. Maybe he and Raylene really did like her."

Shane trudges to his car. The rain is coming down in sheets again. He reaches for the hood of his sweatshirt and, in one fluid motion, pulls it up over his head.

The world around me slows, each raindrop suspended in the air as my mind catapults back to last night.

"Oh my stars," I whisper.

Sage glances at me. "What? You look like you've seen a ghost—and yes, I know that's normal for you, but you know what I mean."

I can't tear my eyes away from Shane. The hood, the build, the way he moves—it's all clicking into place like the world's most unsettling jigsaw puzzle.

"Sage." My voice comes out ragged. "That's the man from last night."

Chapter Nineteen

When she drops me off at home, Sage reaches across the console and grabs my hand. Her tone is light, but her eyes are serious. "What are you going to do?"

"I'm going to look into Shane a bit more. Could be nothing. I mean, lots of people have black sweatshirts."

Her look says she's worried my research might lead me to a killer. "You need to be careful. Call Jones and tell him. Let him handle it."

"All I'm going to do is look into Shane. I swear. Do a little digging into his past. You and Kit can help me at lunch."

She releases my hand. "I'm sorry, but I have to skip lunch. I'm hosting a tea party from one to three. Then Bis and I are finishing recording my inventory after that. Call if you need anything, and don't do anything stupid. If you think Shane is the real culprit who planted that evidence, take it to Jones. Promise?"

"I will, I promise."

As I make my way up the steps to the wraparound porch, the front door swings open before I can reach for the knob. Rosie stands there, worrying her cross pendant. "Betty called and said they're bringing peonies instead of roses because her supplier has a fungus. Not the supplier, the roses. What should we do? Millie Clairmont would sooner die than walk down an aisle without her red roses."

The foyer smells of lemon polish and coffee. I lay my purse on my desk inside my office and hang my drenched jacket on a coat hook. "Tell Betty to come harvest some from Aunt Willa's rose garden. We've got plenty."

Rosie's shoulders relax a fraction. "Good idea. I'll do that. I've got everything else under control for tonight." She ticks off points on her fingers. The church is decorated. The kitchen is stocked for the reception. Paperwork is done." She gives me a triumphant smile. "How was the press conference?"

Moxley moseys in and sniffs me. I must pass the test as he goes to Rosie's desk and joins her chihuahua under it, taking up most of the poor little dog's bed. Fern gives me a forlorn look. "Surprising, but I survived it, and Jones arrested Justin Bowles."

"No!" She slaps a hand to her chest. "He killed Donna?"

"Jones arrested him for entering our house last night and planting evidence. Jury is out about him hurting Donna, but apparently, she had a restraining order out on him for physical abuse."

She reels back. "You're kidding."

"Nope." I sort through the messages she left on my desk. Most are from reporters wanting a statement still. "I think Justin is most likely the murderer."

She makes the sign of the cross and returns to her desk. "By the way, your daddy stopped by to see if you had time to run to the new mercantile store and help him get your mama something for Mother's Day."

Ugh, I've forgotten all about that. No Southern daughter worth her weight in gold would dare forget Mother's Day. I grab my phone and hit speed dial. It goes to voicemail. "Hey, Daddy," I say, "Can you drop by the house for lunch? There's something I want to tell you about, and we can come up with a plan for Mama."

After I disconnect, I grab a coffee and search for Shane online. "Kit's coming over for lunch. She'll probably bring Caboodle. Is that okay?"

"Of course. That kitten is a handful, but she sure is cute."

I'm three pages in on the search engine, having called up a dozen different articles, photos, and other information about Shane and Raylene, when Kit texts me. The kitten has injured its paw, and she has to take it to the vet. She won't make it for lunch.

I'm disappointed, but I assure her that I will talk to her later and ask her to keep me posted on Caboodle's injury.

Several of the posts about Shane and Raylene mentioned their former diner, *Forage*. A description in the menu includes a sentence that I reread several times. Raylene is touted as *a forager who transforms wild foods into culinary dishes*.

Wild foods like *mushrooms*?

"I've got to check on something," I tell Rosie, retrieving my jacket and purse on my way to the door. "The wedding—"

"Will be perfect," she finishes. "Just be careful, okay? You've got that look."

I stop with my hand on the doorknob. "What look?"

"Like you're about to do something dangerous. I'd rather you didn't."

I laugh. "What would I do without you?"

"Crash and burn. Gloriously."

"Too true. I'll be back as soon as I can."

Outside, I think about her words and do the responsible thing. Channeling my inner adult, I pull out my phone and scroll to Detective Jones's number. My thumb hovers over it for a second before I press call. The line rings three, four, five times before his gruff voicemail greeting cuts in. "This is Detective Landon Jones. Leave a message."

No 'please.' No 'I'll call you back.' Just pure, unadorned Jones.

"Detective, it's Ava. I have some information that might be relevant to Donna's murder and my break-in. Please call me back when you receive this. It's about Shane Carter and Raylene Stokes." I catch myself before I say more. "Yeah, just...I'd like for us to discuss it."

I end the call and stare at my phone. Would he deliberately ignore me? *Yes. Yes, he would.* I tap my fingers against the side of my phone, then call the station directly.

"Thornhollow Police Department," a chipper voice answers. It's Officer Melody Parker, fresh out of the academy and still excited about answering phones.

"Hey Melody, it's Ava Fantome-Cross. Is Detective Jones available?"

"Oh, hey, Ava! Sorry, he's tied up right now and said not to disturb him unless the building's on fire." Her voice drops to a whisper. "And even then, he said to try the fire extinguisher first."

Practical as ever. "He's interrogating Justin Bowles?"

"Yep. Been in there about an hour. Looks pretty intense."

As I suspected. But I know what he'd say if I interrupted him to tell him Shane has the same black sweatshirt as my home invader. Or that Raylene most likely knows a toxic mushroom from a nontoxic one. *It's not hard evidence. Only more theories.*

"Do you want to leave a message?" Melody asks.

"Just tell him I called and it's important that I speak to him as soon as possible."

After I hang up, I consider whether confronting Shane or Raylene is a good idea. "What would Daddy do?" He always says good police work is about connecting dots that others don't see as being related.

Dots are all I have. I'll gather more information first, then go to Jones when I have something substantial. Something he can't ignore.

After all, if Shane and or Raylene are involved in Donna's death, then confronting them directly might be dangerous. But observing them? Getting either of them to talk without realizing what I'm after? That I can do.

Still, I'd like backup. Sage is busy, Kit is at the vet, and Rosie has to run things here. I try Logan, but his phone goes straight to voicemail, too. He's probably still with his client.

Brax is up to his eyeballs at The Honey Bar. I call Rhys, but he doesn't answer. The week's guests are no doubt running him ragged.

As a last resort, I dial Daddy's number again. "Change of plans," I tell him. "I could use some of your detective wisdom right now. Could you meet me at the Nottingham Hotel if you're free within the next hour?"

I toss my phone and purse on the passenger seat once I'm inside my car. I glance around for Tabitha, but she's nowhere in sight.

Neither are any ghosts. No Persephone.

Should count my blessings?

The hotel is a twenty-minute drive on a clear day. On a rainy day like today, the potholes are killers, and the road has been known to wash out. The expanse stretches before me, the windshield wipers working furiously.

My mind races with them. If Shane killed Donna, what was his motive? Money? Revenge? If Raylene did it, the same questions hold weight.

But how does Justin Bowles fit into the picture?

How does Bo Remington?

The pieces are there, but they don't fit.

The hotel comes into view, its brick facade and white columns a testament to old Southern money and the pretension that comes with it. I park in the visitors' lot and check my reflection in the rearview.

I plan to start with Baldwin and Kalina and ask them about Shane and Raylene's movements before and after Donna arrived. If I'm lucky, maybe I can speak to the bartender and confirm that Justin was in the bar at the time of the break-in.

And if Shane and Raylene are here?

Well, I'll tackle that when I come to it.

I'm halfway across the parking lot when my phone rings. I fish it out of my purse, squinting at the screen. Unknown number, but it's local. Could be a reporter. I hit accept before I can overthink it. "Hello?"

"Ava? It's Bo Remington."

"Hey, Bo." What does he want? "This is a surprise. Everything okay? You're not backing out of judging, are you?"

"No, nothing like that," he drawls. "I saw the press conference. Wanted to check and see if you're all right."

I pause, stopping next to a decorative planter filled with cheerful but wet-soaked pansies. "That's mighty thoughtful of you. It's been a rough few hours, but I'm fine. You ready for tonight?"

"Good to hear, and yes, I'm ready. You know that honorary judge?"

"Shirley Walker?"

"Is she a voting judge or just there for looks?"

"Does it matter?"

"Well, without Donna's vote, we could end up with a two-way tie, there being just the four of us."

"Oh, I've taken care of that. Mama told me I could ask Raylene to take Donna's place."

There's a beat of silence, then a soft exhale. "Shane will be glad to hear that."

Shane? Not Raylene? "Say, did you know Raylene was a wild foods expert?"

"'Course. That was her original niche. After their diner went bankrupt, she switched to Southern comfort foods."

"Did Justin know about Donna's crush on Shane?"

There's a hitch in his exhale. "I don't know why it would matter. Shane never gave her the time of day, and all that was over by the time she met Justin."

"Shane never returned her feelings, right? That's what you said. At the reception last night, you said the reason she fired him and Raylene was because he wasn't interested in her."

"Why are you asking all these questions?"

"Just curious." I finger one of the flowers, drops of water rolling off of the petals. "I saw Shane leaving The Honey Bar a bit ago. They've set up a memorial for Donna, and he looked sad. It seemed like he was paying respects to someone he cared about."

Bo's pause stretches so long I check my phone to make sure we're still connected. "I'm sure you must be mistaken." His tone is carefully neutral. "He's always been devoted to Raylene."

Devoted enough to kill someone for her?

Or to help her cover it up if *she* killed Donna?

My mind spins.

Bo lowers his voice. "Look, I'm not one to gossip," he says, which in the South means he's about to do exactly that, "but as you already know, Donna had difficult histories with many people."

"And yet Raylene and Shane both speak very highly of her. Why would they do that if she ruined their reputation and caused their diner to go bankrupt?"

"Justin Bowles has been arrested for killing Donna. After the way he treated you, I would think you'd be relieved." A deep breath. "Now, about tonight's preliminary round."

"Thank you for checking on me, Bo." I hang up.

He knows something, but isn't going to tell me. His evasive answers are as good as a confirmation that Shane and

Donna had some kind of history that he doesn't want me digging into. But why?

Inside the lobby, the air conditioning struggles to maintain a cool temperature. People mill about, coming and going from the smaller dining room, the atrium overlooking the back of the property, and the ballroom, where a speaker's voice spills out the doors. A sign on a tripod welcomes visitors to a culinary food co-op class run by Agnes Kepler, owner of a nearby hydroponics farm.

Baldwin is on the phone at the front desk. Kalina is nowhere in sight.

"Ava?"

I turn to see Raylene whisking past with a tray, heading for the ballroom and Agnes' cooking class. My pulse spikes. "Just the person I wanted to see." Not exactly true, but maybe this is my chance to get more intel on her and Shane.

She pauses, then smiles. "Let me deliver this and I'll be right back."

When she returns from the cooking class, I draw her aside. "I have a proposition for you." One brow lifts, suspicious. "With Donna's tragic passing, we're short a judge for the cookoff."

Her expression shifts to one of practiced sympathy, but she doesn't bite. "I saw the news. The press conference. I'm so sorry that man attacked you and besmirched you in public like that. How awful."

That man. Is she putting distance between herself and Justin? I nod solemnly. "It wasn't pleasant, that's for sure. Although that was mild compared to what you went through with Donna."

Her attention skitters away. "You know what they say

about lemons and lemonade. It all worked out for the best in the end." She gestures at the hotel. "I've found a real love for event catering."

"Do you still go foraging?"

The smile falters. Her voice tightens. "What?"

"Foraging. In the woods? For wild edibles?"

She waves a hand, her response a tad too quick. "Oh, no. That was a passing thing. These days, I just want to bring people comfort through food. Now, what were you saying about the judging?"

I allow her to steer us back to safer territory. "We need someone with experience, someone with true culinary expertise." I pause for effect. "Someone like you."

"Me?" Her hand goes to her chest. "Judge the Southern Spirits Cookoff?"

"In Donna's place," I reiterate.

She flicks a look around the room, all faux surprise. It must feel like karmic justice served up on a platter. "Well, I suppose in Donna's memory, it would be my duty to step in. What exactly do you need from me?"

"Be at the fairgrounds at four. The cookoff starts at five. Mama will give us the guidelines and scorecards." I squeeze her arm. "And I do hope Shane won't be upset that I didn't ask him."

A flash of concern crosses her face before she masks it. "Shane? Oh, he won't care. Don't you worry about him." She leans closer, her voice dropping. "Between us? He'll be thrilled."

"Seeing you taking center stage instead of Donna? He should be."

She sighs. "Oil and water, those two."

A revealing comment, despite her attempts at being casual. "I heard she was writing an exposé. One that would do even more damage than her blog had already done to so many small diners and restaurants throughout the South."

Raylene checks her watch. "Goodness, I've got popovers in the oven." She squeezes my hand. "Thank you for this opportunity, Avalon. I won't let you down."

As she bolts for the kitchen, Baldwin hangs up and greets me. I wave at him while watching her go. I still have no hard evidence that proves she and Shane killed Donna, but my gut says she's part of it.

A young man in a black shirt, tie, and slacks rushes past, heading for the bar. I follow him, but Baldwin stops me. "The food fight put us on the news. Did you see it?"

"Sorry, I didn't." From the way he's smiling, I assume it was the good kind of coverage. "Have you had any other spectral troubles?"

"None." He frowns. "Think you could stir things up for us?"

Be careful what you wish for. "Do you mind if I speak to your bartender?"

"Caleb? Why?" He brightens. "Does he have a ghost attached to him?"

"Uh...no." I make up something fast. "A friend wants to enter the Conjured Cocktails & Haunted Sips category of the cookoff. Thought I might pick his brain for ideas."

The phone rings, and Baldwin reaches for the receiver. "Of course. Go ahead."

The bar is dimly lit in that purposeful way that's meant to suggest sophistication rather than hiding weathered features. Brass accents gleam against mahogany, and soft jazz trickles from hidden speakers.

My footsteps falter when I spot Shane hunched over the bar like a man carrying the weight of small-town Georgia on his shoulders. He's nursing a squat glass of amber liquid, his fingers tapping an irregular rhythm against the glass.

I start to turn around and walk out, but what's the worst that can happen? Caleb is here, and I do want to speak to him. Maybe I can draw him out of Shane's hearing.

I straighten my shoulders and approach, channeling my *never let them see you sweat* confidence.

Shane doesn't notice me until Caleb saunters over with a lazy grin. "What can I get you?"

"Sweet tea, please. Extra sweet, extra ice."

"Coming right up."

I start to head to a table far from the bar when Shane says, "You came to the hotel just to order a sweet tea?"

I chuckle, though my heart thuds an irregular beat against my ribs. "Actually, I want to pick Caleb's brain about a drink recipe."

The bartender slides my tea across the polished surface. "For the Conjured Cocktails & Haunted Sips tomorrow? Oh, man. I've got a ton of ideas. In fact, I'm entering one of my personal favorites."

I take the glass and motion for him to follow. "Why don't we talk back there so we don't bother Mr. Carter? I promise not to take much of your time."

"You won't bother me," Shane says, toying with the glass.

Caleb pulls a couple of square cocktail napkins from his back pocket and systematically lays them out on the bar top in front of me, going on and on about the drinks he's created.

I take a stool and drink my tea, trying to act interested. I even occasionally ask a question. *How am I going to get him out of Shane's earshot?*

A couple arrives, and Caleb peels away to wait on them. I'm stuck on a stool two seats from Shane.

It's safe, I tell myself, even though my brain says to run.

"Did she say anything?" Shane asks.

"Sorry?"

"Before she died." He glances at me. "Any final words?"

Like professing her love for him? "No, she didn't." I consider his grief. "I saw you at The Honey Bar after the press conference," I say, watching his face carefully from the corner of my eye. "Were you paying your respects to her?"

His fingers tighten on the glass. "Why would I do that?"

I stir my tea with the straw, ice cubes clinking musically. "So you weren't there for her? You're not sad that she's dead, then?"

Shane takes a swig of his drink, wincing slightly as it goes down. "No matter how I answer that question, you're gonna think I'm a jerk."

"You don't have to pretend with me. I didn't like her either. It's okay to admit that she screwed you and Raylene over, and you're not sorry that she's gone."

His laugh is hollow. "Raylene insists we don't speak ill of her, no matter what."

"Why? She ruined the two of you more than once. You certainly don't owe her any loyalty."

Shane turns to face me fully, suspicion in his eyes. "I thought you were just here for drink ideas."

I offer my most disarming smile. "Do you have any suggestions? I'm doing this research for a friend. I can't enter the contest myself, of course. Oh, and just so you know, Raylene is taking Donna's place as a judge."

For a moment, he seems at a loss for words. "She what?"

I just nod, waiting.

He huffs. "Well, isn't that something? Donna was a tyrant with a near rabid fan base, and here, Raylene Stokes is going to be the judge of your *charming little cookoff*." He says the last three words as if he's bitten into a lemon.

I shift a napkin under my sweating glass, wondering what angle to take here. "You sound bitter."

Another huff. His voice goes cold. "Some things are better left alone. Especially old grudges."

"Shane—"

"I've got to go." He straightens and tosses a tip next to his glass. "Enjoy your tea."

As he walks away, his shoulders are rigid. I stare after him, my drink forgotten and growing watery. I'm not sure whether I feel empowered or guilty for pushing him.

That didn't go as I'd hoped. Instead of answers, I've collected more questions and the distinct impression that Shane is either very afraid or very guilty.

Or both.

Caleb returns. Before he can launch into more advice about the drink recipe I don't need, I ask, "Was Justin Bowles here last night?"

He nods, clearing off Shane's glass. "Sure was. He checked in under a pseudonym, though. You know, a fake name."

I resist the urge to roll my eyes. "I'm aware of what a pseudonym is."

"Yeah, Baldwin figured he didn't want the publicity. He told us staff members to respect that."

"Was Justin alone?"

"For a bit. He was at table six. Then his friend joined him."

I take a casual sip of my watered-down tea. "Did you recognize this friend? Was it Shane, the guy who was just here?"

"No, it was Mr. Remington."

"Bo Remington?"

"Yeah. He's friends with my Uncle Liam. Uncle Liam calls him Remy."

I nearly choke. "*Bo Remington* sat with Justin Bowles?"

"Yes, ma'am. Remy joined him around nine or so. They had themselves a pretty intense conversation. Mr. Bowles drank a lot. Didn't tip, either."

I try to keep my voice steady. "How long were they here?"

"'Bout an hour for Mr. Remington, a little longer for Mr. Bowles."

Hope surges. "Did you happen to hear what they were discussing?"

Caleb gives me a knowing look. "They weren't exchanging pie recipes, I can tell you that."

"Did they mention Donna Dean?"

"A few times." He pockets his napkin recipes and wipes off the counter. "Remy took Mr. Bowles' keys. Said he was too drunk to drive. I thought he knew Bowles was staying here at the hotel, which is why I wasn't monitoring his alcohol intake. Still, I was relieved that he made sure Mr. Bowles couldn't go anywhere on his own."

Yes. This is it. The link I need. "Thanks, Caleb. You've been more helpful than you know." I slide a generous tip across the bar.

He pockets it with a practiced motion. "See you at the cookoff, and if you want any of my recipes..."

I gather my purse. "I'll be in touch. See you tomorrow."

I hurry through the lobby, my sandals clicking against the marble floor. I need to tell Detective Jones about this connection—*now*.

I take out my phone as I push through the revolving door into the sticky midday air. Daddy hasn't arrived, so I text him first, telling him I'm headed home in case he's gotten my previous message. Then I call Jones.

"Come on," I mutter as the phone rings once, twice, three times. "Pick up your phone for once."

The call rolls to voicemail. My skin prickles with a gust of cold air.

Cold air that's completely out of place on this humid Georgia day.

A ghost? A warning?

I don't see anything out of place. I dig for my keys, scanning the distance to my car. Nothing looks out of place. No obvious ghosts hanging around.

Or killers.

But that doesn't mean much in my experience.

The other cars are spread out, the closest one to mind is a blue minivan with a bumper sticker about an honor student.

"Persephone?" I whisper. "Is that you?"

Only silence and a plop of rain answer me.

My fingers close around the keys. The parking lot lights

flicker on as the clouds grow darker, ready to dump a fresh deluge.

I squint, see nothing, and then race for my vehicle. I'm ten feet from it when I hear the scrape of a shoe against pavement behind me.

I stop cold, spin around. I have the keys positioned between my knuckles the way Daddy taught me years ago.

The space behind me appears empty, but the air is heavy, waiting.

"Is someone there?" My voice sounds thin and reedy in the unnaturally still air.

A crow caws from a nearby oak tree, making me jump. More raindrops hit me in the face. Hurriedly, I turn back to the driver's door.

I hit the key fob to unlock it and catch a reflection in the window. A dark figure, moving fast.

I open my mouth to scream, and when I whirl, the scream dies on my lips.

There's no one there.

Movement near the back entrance catches my attention, though.

A tall, lean man in a dark sweatshirt disappears into the hotel.

Shane?

It doesn't matter, I tell myself. It's time to go. I'll tell Detective Jones what I've discovered and let him handle it.

Chapter Twenty

That evening at the fairgrounds, the scent of fried food and sizzling bacon floats on the warm Georgia breeze as I clutch my clipboard. I've told Jones and Daddy everything I uncovered, and I'm focused on staying away from Bo and doing my job as a judge.

I adjust the strap of my sundress, wishing I'd gone for something looser. The fairgrounds are alive with chatter, laughter, and the occasional squeal from kids chasing each other. While we're still working on reviving this place after a tornado destroyed two-thirds of it a few years ago, tonight feels festive. I wish I wasn't too jittery to appreciate it.

"Focus, Ava," I whisper to myself, straightening my posture. A good Southern woman can handle judging a cookoff without passing out or breaking into hives. At least, that's what Mama told me earlier. Speaking of which...

"Move it or lose it!" Mama's voice booms from the security guard's office she's commandeered, nestled near the old cotton candy stand. Inside, wearing her trademark navy-blue linen suit, she's flanked by a tower of scorecards and a harried-looking volunteer who probably regrets signing up for this. Mama's curls have been straightened into a sleek bob, and she bustles around, making sure every judge has their instructions.

"Missy is running late, and we've got fourteen entries competing this year, and our entrants may riot if we fall behind schedule. Avalon, what are you doing just standing there?"

"Sorry," I reply automatically, hurrying toward her like a child caught sneaking cookies before dinner. "I had to speak to Daddy first."

"Here." She slaps a set of scorecards into my hand to tuck into my clipboard. "You're starting with side dishes, along with Raylene. Remember: Smile, nod, and keep your opinions to yourself until you've tried everything twice. And for heaven's sake, don't make faces. These people have been cooking since sunrise."

"Got it," I say, though I'm pretty sure my face naturally contorts when something so much as smells bad.

Mama narrows her eyes, clearly unconvinced. "I mean it. If you insult Mrs. Pruitt's deviled eggs again, we won't hear the end of it till Christmas."

"That was one time, Mama," I protest, though even now, the memory of those overly mustardy monstrosities at the church recital makes my jaw tighten and my stomach churn. "And I was twelve."

"Doesn't matter." She turns me around and gently pushes me toward the main building. The rain stopped, and though there are puddles everywhere, no seems to mind. "Now, go on. The crowd's restless, and your daddy's already had to break up two arguments over who brought the better pimento cheese."

I pulled him aside to tell him about what had happened at the hotel, right after he finished smoothing things over with the two contestants. "Don't worry. He got them all settled."

I want to tell her how nervous I am about Bo, Shane, and Raylene. What I suspect, and that Logan and Daddy already know. Kit and Sage, too. I filled them all in on my interview with the bartender and the mysterious man in the sweatshirt.

But Mama's already barking directions at her volunteer. There's no doubt about it—she's running this show like a well-oiled machine. If anyone can keep this event from spiraling into chaos, it's Dixie Fantome.

The air outside the main building hums with an energy that's equal parts sugar high and small-town pride. The mingling scents of finger foods and side dishes make my stomach grumble despite my nerves. Underlying it all is the tangy scent of cabbage, which does make me scrunch my nose. *Please, Lord,* I pray, *nothing with cabbage.*

Ahead of me, Raylene is talking with a couple of the contestants just inside the open doors. As I enter, they break apart, the contestants rushing to their appropriate booths, smoothing down aprons and rearranging their sample dishes.

"Smile, Ava," Raylene murmurs as she twines her arm with mine to lead me to the first booth. "They can smell fear."

Am I walking together with a killer? "Or maybe that's the sauerkraut." Lordy, I hate sauerkraut.

A plump woman in a sequined apron waves excitedly at

us, nearly knocking over her display of sausage balls in the process. Raylene stops to help her right everything.

Hank Pritchard hollers from the other end of the long line of booths, his suspenders straining with his enthusiasm. "Y'all ready for some good eatin'?"

A cheer rises from the crowd, and I swear someone actually whistles. It's like being at a pep rally but with deviled eggs instead of pom-poms.

"Here we go," I say under my breath, clipboard and scorecards ready. To take my mind off what had happened at the hotel while I waited for Jones to get back to me, I binged six episodes of *Top Grub*, a popular cooking show. We'll see how well I can mimic their famous trio of judges.

Murmurs and gossip make their way to my ears. "That's Dixie Fantome's daughter," someone says. "Bless her heart, she's got big shoes to fill with a mother like that."

"Did you see how much paprika Emma put on her potato salad? Just shameful."

"Is that Logan Cross's wife? She don't look like much of a lawyer's missus, does she?"

Good Lord. I don't look like a judge. I don't look like a lawyer's wife. I focus on walking straight and looking like myself for a change, but my mind keeps drifting back to my talk with Daddy, Logan, and Jones earlier.

"Keep your eyes peeled," Daddy had told me at my kitchen table. "We know Bo Remington and Shane Carter will be at the fairgrounds. If one of them is our guy, we need to keep them distracted so Landon can work his magic."

"Which means searching their vehicles?" Logan had asked. He shook his head. "Walking a tightrope with that, Detective."

Jones hadn't bothered with a scowl, since his face was already set in a permanent one. "You let me worry about that, Mr. Lawyer."

"The point is," Kit had added, "trust your gut, Ava. If something feels off, it probably is. We'll all be there, stationed around the grounds watching those two and Raylene."

"And for anyone in a dark sweatshirt," Logan had added. "We can't rule out it's someone entirely different."

I scan the sea of faces as subtly as I can while pretending to admire a tower of cornbread muffins as I pass. The entrants are too busy fussing over their dishes to notice my attention flicking over the crowd. No sweatshirt in sight yet, but the evening's young.

"Everything alright?" Raylene asks, raising an eyebrow as she joins me.

"Just fine." I smile and stop at the first booth, which is practically a shrine to ghost peppers. Ghost pepper wings, ghost pepper jelly, ghost pepper biscuits. I'm terrified to taste any of it.

Professionalism, Ava. You can't let fear of hot peppers sway you.

"You ready to get started?" Bo drawls, startling me. He's snuck up behind me, holding his clipboard with one hand while the other is stuffed into the pocket of his khakis. His expression is polite, but there's a guarded edge to it that makes me twitch.

"Ready as I'll ever be." I'm glad my voice comes out strong. "But I'll probably need you and Raylene to help me, since this is my first time."

"Nothin' too complicated. Go down your checklist. Add comments—folks like those."

"Comments. Got it." I scribble something vague about presentation on my scorecard as Hailey Robards sets three glasses of milk on the table next to her selection of appetizers.

"It helps smother the fire," she says, pushing a biscuit smeared with jelly toward me.

Raylene has already tasted one and is working on a wing. "This is delicious, Hayley. Subtle heat with lots of other seasonings to balance it out. Is that curry I taste?"

Hayley beams, and the two of them get into a lively discussion.

I nibble the biscuit and down some milk. My tongue feels like it's on fire. "So you and Justin Bowles are friends, huh?" I ask Bo.

Bo blinks, his grip tightening on his clipboard just enough for me to notice. "Oh, I wouldn't say friends. Acquaintances, really. Why?"

I glance over my shoulder. Shane is nowhere to be found. "But you met him at the hotel bar last night."

"Nah, it wasn't me. I had errands to run, then went home early. Quiet night for me."

I bet it was. "Must be nice," I say lightly, though my stomach knots. "Wish I'd had a quiet night myself."

"Yeah, that Justin. I can't believe he did that." He helps himself to the wings and focuses on his scorecard.

Before I can dig deeper, or avoid the revenge of a ghost pepper overload, the sound of heavy boots clomping across the floor draws my attention. I glance over my shoulder and spot Detective Jones striding through the main building.

Daddy keeps pace with him, gesturing animatedly with one hand while clutching his hat in the other.

If Jones and Daddy are here, it means trouble's not far behind.

"Everything alright?" Bo asks, following my gaze.

"Peachy," I lie, plastering on a smile. "Be right back."

"Don't be long. We're moving on to booth two," he says.

As I hurry away, I catch him watching me out of the corner of his eye, and my unease deepens.

Jones and Daddy pull me to a corner out of earshot of the booths and the folks who are watching. "Bowles has been released," the detective says bluntly, his dark eyes boring into mine.

My jaw drops. "Released?"

"His lawyer showed up and I had nothing concrete to hold him on. We found nothing in his car or hotel room."

I heave a sigh. With my luck, Justin will show up here and cause a scene.

"Now," Jones continues, "be careful who you go accusing, alright? This is a murder investigation. Suspicion doesn't equal guilt."

I bristle at his chiding tone. "Believe me. I'm very aware, but I'm telling you, it's either Bo, Shane, or Raylene who killed Donna."

"And I have eyes on all three."

Daddy squeezes my arm. "You focus on the cookoff. We'll handle the suspects."

"Got it," I say, and return to the booth, casting another glance around for Justin. No sign of him or his mob-like fans.

"Carol, I swear, you make the best deviled eggs this side of the Mason-Dixon!" Raylene's voice floats over the crowd, impossible to miss. She's standing at Carol Cooks' booth, her hands fluttering with exaggerated delight as she samples a bite of the woman's entry.

Carol beams, soaking up the praise like a biscuit in gravy. "Why, thank you, sugar. You know I use just a dash of hot sauce for that little kick."

Great, I think, my mouth, throat, and stomach still burning from the ghost pepper nibble. As I swoop by, I down a glass of Hayley's milk. She winks at me.

"Well, it's divine," Raylene declares, placing a delicate hand on her chest as if Carol's deviled egg has reached in and touched her very soul. "Simply divine."

Bo has already moved on to the third booth. I slide up next to Raylene as Missy races up to Hayley's table. Her hair is coming out of its bun, and her skirt is askew. "Sorry I'm late," she says to all of us. "Had a flat tire."

"Flat tire. Mmm-hmm," Raylene murmurs with a humorous glint in her eye. "More like an afternoon rendezvous. Good for her."

I chuckle and find myself hoping that Raylene is innocent. She's kind, a terrific cook, and everyone likes her. *I* like her.

If there's one thing Aunt Willa always taught me, it was to trust my instincts—well, that and never leave the house without lipstick. You never know when you'll run into an ex-boyfriend, she'd say. Is my gut telling me Raylene is innocent, or just that I *want* her to be?

While Missy samples the wings and biscuits, Raylene tempts me with a deviled egg. "What do you think?" she asks as I steel myself for the afterburn.

It's actually quite good. The creamy insides soothe my

throat. I take another bite. Whatever hot sauce Carol used, it's just the right amount, adding flavor without too much heat. "Delicious." I finish it off before I make notes on the scorecard.

Raylene nods. "See?" she says to Carol. "What did I tell you?"

"Good grief," Persephone whispers in my ear, suddenly appearing beside me. "Raylene could charm the devil himself outta his horns, couldn't she?"

"Not now," I hiss, keeping my eyes on my scorecard. Raylene says something to Carol, and the two of them laugh.

"Don't get your girdle in a twist."

Easy for her to say. She doesn't have to juggle ghosts, murder suspects, and the mayor for a mother.

She floats a few feet away. "I just wanted you to know Justin Bowles is on his way here."

Before my stomach can drop, a loud crash echoes across the building, followed by a chorus of raised voices. I whip around to see a table near the center of the room tipped over, a cascade of tea and other drinks spilling onto the floorboards. A young woman in an apron is frantically trying to save what's left of her display, while a toddler wails nearby, clutching a sticky fistful of what I assume was once a cupcake.

I glance around for Mama, knowing she'll want to handle this before it turns into a full-blown spectacle. She must be in the other section of the building, setting up for tomorrow's main event.

"Excuse me, pardon me," I murmur, weaving through the throng of people with as much grace as I can muster. Daddy's nowhere in sight. Neither is Jones.

Neither are Logan or my friends.

That's when I know something's wrong.

While I keep an eye on Bo, they're all out watching for Shane.

When I can't locate Mama anywhere in the building, I head to the security guard's office. "Mama?" I call out, peeking inside. The air smells faintly of stale coffee, but the room is as empty as a church on Super Bowl Sunday. "Well, shoot," I mutter, the door creaking shut behind me.

Before I can even think about heading back out, something moves—a shadow flickering in the frosted glass of the door. My breath catches. Every hair on my arms prickles like static electricity. A hand clamps down hard on my shoulder, its grip cold and unyielding.

"Hey!" I yelp, twisting instinctively to break free. But an arm snakes around my waist, pulling me back against a body that feels like it was carved out of granite. Panic floods my veins as I thrash and kick, my shoes scuffing against the linoleum floor. "Let go of me! What in the—"

"Quiet," a low voice growls in my ear.

Quiet? Oh, bless their heart if they think I'm gonna cooperate with that demand.

"Get your grimy paws off me!" I yell, flinging an elbow backward and catching the man somewhere solid. There's a grunt of pain, satisfying but fleeting, as his grip tightens like a vise. My mind spins as I claw at his arm, nails scrabbling against soft fabric.

A sweatshirt.

"Help!" I shout, my voice cracking under the weight of fear. "Somebody help me!"

"Shut up!" the voice hisses again, and this time, I feel

something sharp press against my ribs. A knife? Oh, sweet Lord above, this just went from bad to worse.

My pulse roars in my ears as I freeze for half a second, long enough for him to drag me toward the door.

I summon every ounce of fight left in me and stomp down hard on his foot, the heel of my sandal connecting with what feels like a steel-toed boot. Dang it. He lets out another grunt, but it's not enough to make him loosen his hold.

"Fine," I say through gritted teeth, "you wanna play rough, Justin?" I'm guessing it's him or Shane. "Let's play rough." I swing my head backward, aiming for his nose. It's not graceful, but he doesn't expect it. He grunts and swears. It buys me enough wiggle room to twist halfway out of his grasp.

"Help!" I scream again as I bolt for the door, adrenaline and pure desperation propelling me forward. My ankle wobbles in my sandal, and I nearly topple over, but I catch myself and keep running. The fairgrounds blur into a whirl of colors and noise as I barrel toward the main building.

There's no one out here to hear me, though. They're all inside the building.

A strong hand grabs the back of my dress and yanks. I stumble, gasping, and then another hand clamps around my mouth, smothering my cries.

"Enough," the voice snarls, low and venomous, as I'm hauled backward like a rag doll. My legs kick uselessly, my sandals flying off in opposite directions. Tears sting my eyes as the world tilts sideways.

Chapter Twenty-One

I'm thrown down and land hard on a sticky, grimy floor. My knees scrape painfully on the concrete, and my head smacks into a cabinet. My breath whooshes out in a rush, and for a moment, I can't tell which way is up, my vision swimming from the blow.

The air is layered with the scent of burnt oil and stale popcorn, with a faint undercurrent of what might be ketchup. I push myself up to all fours, trying to get a grip—literally and figuratively. I press my palms into the dusty floor and wince at the sharp edge of what feels like a rogue nacho chip digging into my skin.

Popcorn, ketchup, and nachos? The old concession stand? It hasn't been used since last year's fair. It looks almost identical to the security guard's office, but is packed with shelves for prepackaged foods, a freezer, fridge, and a soda fountain.

I blink, trying to focus, but the dim light filtering through the slatted windows isn't doing my wonky vision any favors.

The door is behind me now, closed. The only other exit is a narrow window too high up and way too small for anything bigger than a squirrel.

A shadow shifts, falling over me, and my stomach does a backflip worthy of an Olympic medal. I lift my gaze, dragging my eyes up from the scuffed tips of two very solid boots to the hulking form of not one, but two men standing over me.

"Well, there you go," I say, coming to my bare feet and brushing dirt off my dress. I have to grab the cabinet to steady myself. "I was right. At least partially."

Shane Carter shakes his head. He's wearing his Forage t-shirt again. I can't make out who's behind him. "You're just too nosy for your own good."

I lick my lips and try to think of a way to get past him. Or buy time. But what good will that do? Who's going to look for me here? *Nope, my escape is all on me.* "You poisoned Donna."

He gives me a grin that's off. "Raylene did that."

Something about that grin doesn't sit right. "I don't believe you. She wouldn't do that to anyone, not even an enemy."

The second man slides to Shane's right and spits on the floor, not far from my feet. Justin Bowles. He's wearing a shirt that promotes his blog. "So now you're an expert on Raylene? You should have stuck to being the pampered mayor's daughter and kept your nose out of this. It was none of your business."

"It became my business when that poor woman died right in front of me." I inventory my surroundings. *I need a weapon. Anything.* "She may not have been a very nice person, but there's no excuse for what you did."

"Donna tried to ruin us," Justin says. "We ain't about to let you take her place, on screen or in court."

The counters are empty, and outside of bagged chips in a wire display, there's nothing worth throwing. I doubt potato chips will have much effect on deterring my captors. *Persephone*, I call silently. *Help!*

I shuffle a few steps back, running into the soda machine. Doubtful there's any soda in the lines, and even if there were, what good would it do? "There are better ways to fight people like Donna than murder. Legal ways."

Shane flashes the knife, looking sad. "Not everything can be resolved with lawsuits."

Stall them. "Like broken hearts?" I ask.

"Quiet," he snaps, his jaw tight enough to crack a pecan. He's all sharp edges and bad intentions, his face a mask of something that teeters between guilt and outright panic.

Justin continues to hover behind him, looking like he might bolt if someone so much as sneezes too loudly. His eyes dart around the cramped space, landing everywhere but on me.

My heart's pounding so hard I'm surprised they can't hear it. The fluorescent light flickers above us, casting weird shadows across their faces. For a split second, Shane looks almost ghostly, but there's nothing supernatural about the knife glinting in his hand.

"Alright, alright." I raise my hands in mock surrender. My fingers tremble, but I keep my voice steady. "No need to get all dramatic. Let's just talk this out like civilized folks, okay? Maybe over a MoonPie?" I glance toward the shelf beside me, where the little marshmallow sandwiches sit neatly stacked, as though oblivious to the fact they're witnessing a potential hostage situation.

"Stop joking around," Shane says, his voice sounding flat, dead. "You don't know who you're messing with."

"Oh, please." I keep my tone as even as I can manage. "I think the better question is whether you know who *you're* messing with." My eyes lock onto his, and for a moment, I swear I see him flinch—but maybe that's just wishful thinking. "Everyone knows Raylene wouldn't hurt a fly unless it landed on her sweet tea. You poisoned Donna." I shift my attention to Justin. "Or did you do it?"

"Raylene—" Shane cuts off, glaring at me like I'm the one with a knife. His jaw works overtime like he's chewing on something tough. Guilt, maybe? Or another lie? "Donna ruined her. Us. Raylene cried for days. She was devastated."

"Devastated isn't the same as homicidal," I fire back, stepping closer despite every nerve in my body screaming at me to stay put. I'll be darned if I let Shane see me flinch. "Start telling the truth, or so help me, I'll haunt you when this is over."

"Shut up!" He looks like he's going to backhand me, and I flinch back, but he stops himself. "You're right, okay? Raylene didn't know. I—I did it."

I glance at Justin, whose face has gone pale. He's full of bluster, but he's not a killer. "Really?" My eyebrows shoot up in question. "You? You had the balls to do such a thing?"

"Yes, me!" He takes a menacing step forward, but I hold my ground. "Donna ruined everything. Raylene was miserable because of her, and I couldn't stand to see it anymore. So, yeah, I figured out a way to make her pay. I knew about the mushrooms. Learned about them back when Raylene was still into foraging. I planted that bag at your place to throw Jones off the trail."

"And you played along with making Justin look like he did it." I glance at Justin. "That wasn't part of the plan, though, was it, Justin? Shane threw you under the bus."

Justin isn't the sharpest tool in the shed, only now seeming to catch on. He grabs Shane's arm. "You were framing me by making it look like I framed her?"

Shane waves the knife like some deranged orchestra conductor. "She's lying. Don't believe her."

"You're playing all the angles, aren't you, Shane?" I make a tsking noise. "You profess your love for Raylene, but if push comes to shove, you'll do the same to her, won't you? You'll claim she put those mushrooms in Donna's breakfast sandwich in order to save your own neck."

Shane glowers. "Better her than me."

And there it is. I'm staring down Donna's killer. "There's still one thing I don't get," I say. "What does Bo Remington have to do with all this?"

"Bo?" Shane mutters, glancing at Justin like he's hoping for backup. Justin shrugs, hands shoved deep into his pockets, clearly not up for playing accomplice of the year. Mr. Bluster from this morning is a coward tonight. "Donna crushed him. She humiliated him in front of half the town." Shane's voice is low now, almost bitter, and it sends a chill skittering down my spine.

Let him talk. Buy time. "Why do you care?"

He snorts and shakes his head like I just don't understand. "His whole life, Bo wanted to be a famous chef. Applied to work for her after she fired me and Raylene. She put him through the wringer. Made him jump through every hoop, then told everyone his cooking was garbage. Called his shrimp and grits 'an insult to Southern cuisine.' Said he should stick to his day job. The guy was destroyed. His dream was destroyed."

Just like Raylene. He doesn't say the words, but his point is clear. "Destroyed enough to join you in a murder plot? That doesn't sound like him."

"Sometimes people snap," Shane retorts. "And Bo...he wanted to prove her wrong. Show her what it felt like to lose everything. It wasn't hard to get him on board once I laid out the plan."

"So you've got revenge, heartbreak, and culinary aspirations gone awry. Sounds like the plot of a really bad Hallmark movie."

He slams the hilt of the knife against the counter. The sound ricochets through the cramped concession stand, and for a second, even Justin flinches. "This isn't a joke! Donna ruined all of us. All. Of. Us."

"Shane," Justin cuts in, finally finding his voice. "What are we going to do with her?"

"Just...give me a minute," he snarls, shooting him a glare. "I need to think."

"She knows everything now. You told her everything."

Shane flashes the knife at him. "I know that, moron."

"Whoa, whoa, whoa!" I raise my hands. "No one else needs to get hurt. We can work this out with Detective Jones."

"No we can't!" Shane returns his attention to me. He

takes another step closer, and I instinctively back up, bumping into a shelf stacked with boxes for popcorn.

"Okay, hold on," I say quickly, keeping my hands raised like I'm surrendering in some old Western. "Do you really want to add another murder to your rap sheet?"

"Better than going to jail," he says simply, and the hard gleam in his eyes makes my stomach twist.

When he lunges, I do the only thing I can think of—I grab the nearest weapon-like object. My hand closes around a jumbo-sized can of nacho cheese sauce. Not exactly Excalibur, but desperate times call for processed dairy. "Back off!" I yell, swinging it with all my might. The jar connects with his forearm, but it doesn't knock the knife out of his grip.

"Nice try," he growls.

I reach for something else—a plastic tray. I hurl it at Justin, who's trying to maneuver behind me. It bounces harmlessly off his chest and clatters to the floor.

My hands dart around blindly, grabbing a candy bar. A packet of mustard. A tin of breath mints. I toss them one after another, none of them having much effect except to make Shane even angrier as he bats them away.

"Enough!" He surges forward. His free hand shoves me hard, and I stumble back, catching the edge of the soda machine to steady myself. For a split second, I think I'm going to get away with just a bruise—then he swipes at me with the knife.

Pain blooms hot and sharp across my upper arm. "Ow! You son of a biscuit-eating bulldog!" I yelp, clutching the wound as blood seeps through my fingers. It's not deep, but it stings like the dickens, and I suddenly understand why people always scream in slasher movies.

"Hold her!" he orders Justin.

Justin hesitates a moment before stepping toward me with a look of reluctant determination. If only I could break him. My mind scrambles for some kind of plan, but all I can think about is how ridiculous it is that I might meet my end in a place that smells like stale popcorn and overcooked pretzels.

The air shifts without warning, like the moment before a summer thunderstorm. There's a faint pop, followed by a series of louder bangs as bags of chips start exploding off the shelves. Doritos. Fritos. Lays. They're all airborne, pelting Shane and Justin in a barrage of salty vengeance.

"What the—" Shane ducks, swatting at a rogue bag of barbecue chips that smacks him square in the face.

"Is this... Is this you?" Justin asks, wide-eyed as a bag of gummy worms sails past his head.

"Do I look like I have telekinetic snack powers?" I shout back, equally baffled but starting to feel the tiniest flicker of hope.

The soda machine chooses this moment to join the fray, letting out a high-pitched *whirrrrr* before erupting like a fizzy geyser. Five kinds spray everywhere, drenching the room in sticky sweetness.

Shane slips first, his feet skidding out from under him as he lands unceremoniously on his back. Justin isn't far behind, flailing like a baby deer on ice before toppling over with a loud thud.

Chips continue to rain down like confetti, and the soda machine gurgles ominously as if daring anyone to come near it. Somewhere in the chaos, I catch the faintest whiff of perfume—gardenias. Then I see the outline of a woman.

"Donna," I murmur, a mix of relief and exasperation bubbling up in my chest. "It's good to see you, even if you're turning me into a snack bag survivor."

She disappears.

Okay, then. I don't think. I just move. Coming out of my crouch on the sticky mess of soda and floor grit, I bat away the chaos of Donna's ghostly snack attack swirling around me. My ribs protest—thank you, mystery wound—but I grit my teeth and bolt for the door like a cat being chased off a porch. I slip slightly as my bare feet skid across the wet concrete.

"Stop her!" Justin yells, his voice cracking with panic. I don't dare look back. Frankly, I don't care if they're slipping on chips or doing synchronized swimming in the cola puddle. All I know is that I've got one shot at escape.

Even as small as the space is, the concession stand door feels a million miles away. Somehow, miraculously, I reach it. My fingers fumble with the handle—it's greasy, yuck—but I shove it open, and the humid Georgia night air slaps me in the face.

My legs feel like Jell-O, and I swear the ground moves up to meet me faster than it should. One second, I'm running, and the next, I'm face-first in the dirt, spitting out what tastes suspiciously like clay.

Somewhere behind me, there's a loud crash followed by a string of colorful curses. "Get back here, you nosy little—" Shane's words are swallowed by the sound of his boots pounding against the gravel. He's gaining on me fast. My pulse jackhammers in my ears, drowning out everything but the primal instinct screaming one word over and over: *Run.*

My legs don't want to work right, though. Desperation lights a fire under me, and I twist around just as he reaches out to grab me. Without thinking, I lash out with my foot, aiming for the sweet spot all Southern mamas warn their sons about in gym class.

My heel connects with a satisfying thwack.

"Gah!" He doubles over, clutching himself and letting loose a guttural groan that sounds like a dying possum. He stumbles back a step—or three—and I waste no time scrambling to my feet again, adrenaline coursing through me like I just downed a double-shot espresso.

"Ava!" Logan's voice slices through the cool night air, and I nearly collapse again, this time out of pure relief. My very own Southern knight in shining loafers is sprinting toward me. Behind him, Detective Jones and Daddy follow, each wearing expressions that could curdle milk.

"Here!" I croak, waving weakly. My hand feels like it weighs forty pounds. "Hurry!"

Logan reaches me first, sliding to his knees beside me and gripping my shoulders like I might evaporate into thin air. "What on God's green earth—" His voice falters as his eyes drop to the blood soaking the side of my shirt. "You're hurt."

I pant, clutching at his arm. "Shane... Justin... they're—" I hiccup a noise that sounds like a sob. "And Bo Remington. They're all in on it."

Daddy barrels past us. Jones makes me repeat myself. The two of them then descend on Shane, who's still doubled over like a busted lawn chair, while Justin makes a break for it.

"Don't even think about it, son," Daddy barks, and then hits him with a taser. Justin's body goes rigid, and he drops to his knees.

"They did it," I mutter, sagging against Logan as the fight drains out of me. He wraps an arm around my shoulders, steadying me. "They poisoned Donna."

"Let's get you up," he says gently as he studies my face. "Jones and Nash can handle these two fools."

'Handle' might be a strong word for what the two friends are doing—Jones looks about as thrilled to be here as a cat at a dog park—but between him and Daddy, they've got Shane and Justin wrangled and cuffed in no time.

"Landon, you want me to call for backup?" Daddy asks, pulling out his phone.

"Please." Jones scowls. "And then take care of your daughter."

The familiar scent of lavender wafts over me before I even see her. Sage appears at my side like she's materialized out of thin air, her braid swinging over one shoulder. Kit's right behind her, dragging poor Raylene along like a reluctant puppy. And then there's Mama, marching for me and clutching a clipboard.

People flood out of the main building and hurry to see what all the hubbub is about.

"Lord have mercy," Mama says, eyeing the blood on my shirt and picking chip pieces from my hair. "What happened? You look like you've been in a deadly food fight."

"Thanks, Mama," I manage, coughing out a laugh despite myself. "Really needed that boost to my self-esteem."

"Raylene Stokes," Jones says, pointing a finger so

accusatory it would make Mama jealous. "Did you know about this?"

"About what?" Raylene echoes, gesturing wildly toward the scene—the blood on my shirt, the cuffs on Shane, the whole mess.

Jones looks as if he wants to shake her. "The poisoning of Donna Dean by these men."

Her voice is high-pitched and shaky, like a tea kettle on the verge of boiling over. "No! Absolutely not! I swear, I don't know what's going on!"

"Save it for the station," Jones grunts, jerking his head toward her. "You're coming in for questioning."

"Questioning?" Raylene squeaks, looking like she might faint dead away. "But I— Ava, I swear I didn't have anything to do with this...whatever this is."

"Don't forget Bo," I say when I see him peeking over some heads of the gathering crowd.

"Got him." He points to someone—Brax—and the next thing I see is my best friend taking Bo down to the ground and shoving his foot in Bo's back to hold him there.

There's a lot of commotion and folks talking over each other, but Jones has all three men lined up near the exit gate in record time, thanks to Daddy and Brax.

"Come on." Logan places a gentle arm around my waist to lead me past them. "We need to get you to Doc."

"I'm fine," I protest weakly, though the sharp pain in my side says otherwise. I look down and realize that Shane cut my belly as well. Warm blood seeps through my dress in a scarlet bloom. "Or not."

"Come on." Daddy gestures for me and Logan to follow him. "Let's go."

My legs feel like boiled spaghetti, but with Logan's arm around me, I manage to stay upright. "Fine, but then I need some wine and pizza."

"I'm on it," Kit says with a wink. "Caboodle and I are at your service."

I smile and head to the clinic to get stitched up.

Chapter Twenty-Two

The following morning, Logan promises to make me breakfast after my shower. I already took two long, hot showers last night after getting stitched up, but I need another this morning. I'm not sure if I'm still trying to remove the soda and blood or the lingering stress, even though Shane, Justin, and Bo are all in jail.

When we get downstairs, Moxley at our heels and the cats crying and weaving around our ankles, demanding their breakfast before anything else, we stop short just inside the doorway.

"Well, would you look at that." I blink at the scene before us.

On the table, propped up against the recipe tin, is Birdie's Blessing Pie recipe. Her unmistakable printing almost lifts off the yellowed paper as if she's still alive and jotting it down this very moment. On the counter, every ingredient is neatly laid out: sugar, flour, butter, and fresh peaches so ripe they practically glow.

"Someone's been busy," Logan says. He moves to the coffee pot without missing a beat, already pulling out the canister of beans. "Guess she didn't want you slacking this morning."

"Guess not," I reply, stepping closer to inspect the setup. The measuring cups are stacked in perfect size order, and the rolling pin rests at an angle on the countertop, like it's waiting for me to pick it up and get moving. "She wants me to take it to the cookoff."

"Did she tell you that?"

I reach out cautiously, half expecting the flour to poof into smoke or the peaches to vanish the moment I touch them. But no, everything stays solid and real under my fingers. A lump forms in my throat. "She didn't have to."

"Should you call Queenie to help you? You're not exactly...a baker," Logan teases. The machine hums to life when I shoot him a glare, filling the air with the rich, nutty scent of the fresh grounds.

When the grinding stops, I grab a set of mixing bowls. "With Birdie's help, I'm not only going to bake this to perfection, but it's going to bring in top bids at the silent auction today."

"You're entering it in the auction?" His hair is still mussed from sleep, and he's wearing the kind of grin that comes from knowing way too much about your wife's cooking pitfalls. "Is that a good idea?"

"Careful, Cross," I warn, waving a wooden spoon in his direction. "Don't make me sic Birdie on you."

"Please. She already likes me better than you," he says with a wink.

I set to work on the pie, and Logan feeds our pets, then

steals one of my bowls to crack eggs into it for breakfast. He glances my way, sees my somewhat befuddled expression as I try to decide what to do first. "This should be interesting."

I shake my head, fighting a smile, and turn back to the recipe. It's not complicated—Birdie believed in letting ingredients speak for themselves—but there's a certain reverence required when handling something as legendary as her Blessing Pie. I'm sore and tired, having not slept much, but I'm alive and that's something of a blessing in itself.

I measure the flour and sugar carefully while Logan moves around behind me, setting bacon to sizzle in the cast iron skillet and humming to an old country tune on the radio. Between the smell of brewing coffee and the gentle clatter of utensils, the kitchen feels alive. Like Birdie herself is hovering just out of sight, arms crossed and watching to make sure I don't skimp on the butter.

"How's it coming?" Logan asks over his shoulder, flipping the bacon.

"Don't rush me," I reply, squinting at the instructions. "This pie's supposed to bring blessings, remember? Can't rush blessings."

"True that," he concedes, sliding two mugs onto the counter and pouring coffee. He hands me one without looking, like he's done a thousand times before, and I take it gratefully.

For a moment, we're quiet, the only sounds the crackle of bacon and the soft scrape of my spoon mixing flour and sugar when I commence again. It's peaceful, cozy—the kind of morning that makes you forget for a second about ghosts and mysteries and anything heavier than breakfast.

"Hey," Logan says suddenly, breaking the silence.

"Think Birdie ever thought about adding cinnamon to this pie?"

"Logan Cross," I gasp, clutching the wooden spoon dramatically to my chest. "You take that blasphemy right out of this kitchen."

"Just saying." He grins as he turns back to the stove. "A little cinnamon never hurt anybody."

The creak of the back door swinging open interrupts my focus on folding butter into flour, and I glance up to see Tabitha step into the kitchen like she owns the place. Given that she founded the town, she kind of does.

Today, her mass of red hair is pulled back in a loose braid and she's dressed in what I can only describe as "Victorian farm chic." The clothes all came from my closet, and yet, she pulls them together in unusual ways that look dignified, whereas if I tossed on that combination of skirt, top, and gloves, I'd look like a child playing dress-up.

She pauses to snatch a piece of bacon as her eyes zero in on the pie ingredients scattered across the counter.

"Butter," she declares approvingly, peeling off the gloves one finger at a time. "Birdie always insisted blessings stick best when there's plenty of butter."

"Morning to you, too," I say dryly, elbow-deep in dough crumbs. "You knew Birdie? Why didn't you tell me?"

She strides over to the counter with all the regal authority of someone who was once worshipped for her ability to make sheep behave. "Now, now," she says in that lilting Scottish accent of hers, "don't get cheeky with your great-granny, lass." She leans in to inspect the recipe card propped against the tin. "I didn't know her personally, but her reputation spread far and wide."

"Well, it sounds like she did have a penchant for flair." I brush flour off my hands. "Did you come by to critique, or are you here to help?"

"Help, obviously." She rolls up her sleeves in dramatic fashion. "If you're going to do this right, it'll take a Holloway touch. You've got raw talent, Ava, but baking 'tis not your best skill."

"Honest as ever," I mutter, nudging a mixing bowl toward her and ignoring Logan's laugh.

We settle into a rhythm, passing ingredients back and forth as the morning sunlight filters through the lace curtains. Tabitha chills the dough while I peel peaches with more enthusiasm than skill. It's oddly comforting, baking with my many-times-removed grandmother who also happens to be occasionally turn herself into a cat.

I reach for the pie plate and my stitches pull, making me wince. My thoughts spin back to last night and Shane's knife.

Tabitha has a habit of reading my mind. At least, it always seems that way. "Careful," she warns, and retrieves the pie plate from the high shelf for me. "Keep your thoughts positive or it might turn the pie bitter." She slides a small jar of amber liquid toward me. "A splash of vanilla. Trust me. It's not in Birdie's recipe, but I promise she won't haunt us for it."

"How do you know?" I ask, eyeing her suspiciously.

She gives a sly smile. "Because she borrowed my short-bread recipe that had been handed down through several generations and added nutmeg without asking. Turnabout's fair play."

I laugh, pouring a careful splash into the bowl of

peaches. The scent blossoms instantly, warm and sweet. "But if this pie ends up cursed, I'm blaming you."

"Deal." She pats my shoulder. "Though we both know if it brings blessings, I'll take full credit."

"Naturally." I shake my head. "Typical witch."

"Typical grandchild," she counters, grinning.

And just like that, the pie starts to feel like more than dessert. It takes on its own kind of magic.

We enjoy breakfast while the dough chills, and Samuel joins us, even though his ghostly form can't enjoy bacon or biscuits. We're discussing the recipes when it happens—a soft, cool breeze brushes the back of my neck. I freeze and glance at Tabitha. "Did you feel that?"

"Feel what?" she replies without looking up from her eggs, her tone far too casual.

I gesture vaguely to the air around us. "A chilly breeze."

"Maybe Birdie's checking in," she says with a shrug.

"Birdie?" I venture softly.

There's no reply, no sudden apparition in a floral apron offering unsolicited pie-making advice.

"She's probably just observing," Tabitha offers. "Making sure we donna mess up her recipe."

While the men clean up the dishes, I retrieve the crust and pick up the rolling pin. "Well, if she's here, I wish she'd give me some feedback on this crust. Is it too dry? Too sticky?"

"Try talking to her," Tabitha suggests. "What's the worst that could happen?"

"Knowing our luck? The oven will explode," Logan deadpans.

I waggle the rolling pin in his direction. "I'm going to run you out of the kitchen if you keep that up."

Tabitha and Samuel leave, but Rosie arrives, her hair pulled back into a loose ponytail and a thermos clutched in her hand. She looks every bit the Southern belle, trying to survive on caffeine and charm alone. "Morning, y'all," she chirps, nodding to all of us. "Thought I'd stop by and make sure you're still breathing after yesterday."

"Still breathing," I confirm, easing the crust into the pie dish. "Barely moving, but breathing."

"Good Lord, Ava. You do attract trouble." She eyes me with mock horror. "I couldn't believe it when Brax caught up with me after the wedding." She peers at the pie dish as I fold the peach filling into it. "And now you're baking?"

"Birdie's Blessing Pie. I thought it appropriate for the silent auction."

She sets her thermos on the counter and leans against it. "You need anything? Coffee? Aspirin? A new body?"

"All of the above." I plunk chunks of cold butter in with the peaches, just like the recipe says to. I scrape dough from my fingers. "But seriously, how was the ceremony last night? Everything go okay?"

"Smooth as silk." Her expression relaxes into a satisfied smile. "No wardrobe malfunctions, no drunk uncles doing the chicken dance—though I think I saw one trying to flirt with the fondue fountain."

"Small miracles," Logan says, drying our breakfast dishes and putting them away.

"Exactly," Rosie agrees. "Now, I better not keep you too long. I'll see you at the cookoff later. The kids are excited for the petting zoo, and I need to buy strawberry bread at the church ladies' booth. Looks like your Mama got the nice weather she ordered."

Of course she did.

I get the pie in the oven before the back screen opens, and Rhys comes in wearing a lopsided grin with a to-go coffee cup in hand. "Are you baking?" His voice comes out two octaves too high. "Guess it's a good thing I stepped over."

"Yes, I'm baking." I give an exaggerated sigh. "Don't be rude."

He and Logan exchange glances. "Figured I'd check in on you after yesterday." He takes in the mess I've made. "Did you hit your head? Is that why you're baking?"

"I *did* hit my head, but it didn't affect my brain. I'm doing this for Birdie."

"Blessing pie?" Rhys reads the recipe. "Did she ask you to do it?"

"She did, in fact."

He pauses, then looks at me directly. "How're you holding up? You look better than I expected—no offense."

"Gee, thanks." I snort, though I can tell he means well. "I'm fine, really. Just trying to get this thing together. Tabitha helped, so if it's terrible, I'm blaming her."

Both men chuckle, and Logan leaves to check his voicemail.

"Smart." Rhys plunks down at the table. "I get the first slice."

"I'm putting it in the silent auction with a copy of the recipe," I tell him. "It should bring in some money for the charity."

"Haunted pies. Now that's a niche market." He freezes, his eyes narrowing as he points frantically. No words come out of his mouth for several seconds. "Uh... Ava? Is that... Birdie?"

I follow his gaze. The wooden spoon in the empty mixing bowl slowly turns as if guided by an invisible hand.

"Birdie," I say, setting the timer on the oven. "Don't scare the guests."

"I'm not good with ghosts," Rhys tells her, speaking to thin air. "They freak me out. But, girlfriend, I love your recipes!"

"Speaking of Birdie..." I trail off, sitting down at the table. Logan returns and pours fresh coffee for both of us before he joins me and Rhys. "Doc and the medical examiner finally finished her autopsy."

The kitchen goes quiet, save for the faint hum of the fridge and the occasional creak of the old floorboards. Logan strokes my back. "What did they discover?"

Doc had shared the news while stitching me up. "Turns out, there were signs of trauma to her neck and a hairline fracture along the base of her skull consistent with a fall."

"So she wasn't murdered?" Rhys asks.

I'm not so sure. "Doc wouldn't speculate, but he shared what the ME said. She was most likely shoved, pretty hard, too. She tripped, fell, and smacked her head on something solid."

"Possibly an accident," Logan says, "but more likely not."

"That's awful." Rhys's brow furrows in genuine concern. "Who would do something like that? Birdie was beloved, wasn't she?"

"She was." I nod, feeling a pang of sadness for her. "But people have secrets. Even in Thornhollow. Maybe especially in Thornhollow."

"Is there anything we can do?" Rhys asks.

I exhale deeply. "I have an idea, and I'm not letting her story end like this. We're going to honor her today. With this pie, with the charity, with everything. She deserves that much."

"Well," Rhys says, his voice lighter. "I'm at your disposal."

Twenty minutes later, the pie is cooling, and I'm on the phone with the president of Birdie's charity.

"Hi, Mrs. Bradley? It's Ava Fantome-Cross. I was wondering—would it be possible to pick up Lorna Duval and bring her to the closing ceremony tonight? If she's up to it, I think she should be there." My heart flutters nervously as I pace the kitchen, waiting for the response.

"Of course," Mrs. Bradley says. "That's a wonderful idea, Ava. Birdie would be touched. I'll check with Lorna's caregivers at the nursing home and see if I can make the arrangements."

"Thank you." I hang up and glance at the pie, then at Logan and Rhys.

"Alright, team." I clap my hands. "Let's go make Birdie proud."

Chapter Twenty-Three

The fairgrounds are alive with a sea of folding chairs, picnic tables, and red-and-white checkered tablecloths flapping in the breeze. Tents line the area around the main building, each one festooned with bunting, banners, or the occasional plastic pig wearing sunglasses. Somewhere to my left, someone's got a banjo, and there's a toddler stomping around in cowboy boots, yelling, "Yeehaw!"

"Well," Logan says, brushing imaginary lint off his crisp white polo, "if this isn't the most Southern thing I've seen in some time." He grins, and adjusts the brim of his baseball cap. "You sure you're up for this after what happened last night?"

"Hey, y'all!" Bailey, the librarian and my co-president of the Chamber, waves from behind her booth, which is selling used books to raise funds for our children's section. She's wearing a hat shaped like a giant peach because why not? It's from one of our Peachy Reads storytimes. Everything about today is as loud and proud as Georgia itself.

"Selling much?" I call.

"We've made over fifty dollars already!"

"Nice!" She asks about my health and I assure her I'm back to normal. It's not quite true, but close enough.

We pass the petting zoo and ladies' auxiliary booths, where half the church choir is gathered, singing and clapping to draw folks in. Before I can soak in much more, I hear the unmistakable sound of Daddy's voice cutting through the din. "Ava! Logan!"

He strides over to us with his pale green shirt tucked so neatly into his jeans, you'd think he was heading to Sunday service instead of a cookoff. He's holding his ball cap in one hand, fanning himself. "How are you doing?" he asks as he kisses my cheek.

"Happy to be here."

"Good thing. Raylene's backed out. Your mama is scrambling for judges."

My voice comes out in a screech, and half the fairground turns to look at me. "Raylene did *what*?"

He snugs his cap on. "She called this mornin' and said she can't judge. It wouldn't be right after what happened."

Jones told us last night that the state's attorney had offered a deal to the three men. Bo and Justin turned on Shane, who then confessed. Jones had gathered enough evidence to confirm that Raylene was innocent, and he'd let her go.

Still. This puts us in a real pickle. And not the baby gherkin kind.

Daddy touches my shoulder. "You're one of the last judges standing. If you're up for it."

My stomach bottoms out. It's just me and Missy now. And I still don't have a clue what to do.

"Don't panic," Daddy says. "If you don't want to do it, your mother will freak, but she'll find someone to take your place."

I can't leave Mama in a lurch. "I can and will do it," I insist, trying to sound confident.

The woman in question, the legend who is my mother, sweeps past us, giving me the once-over without a word about my clothes, makeup, or hair. She hugs me and drags me away from Logan toward the main building. "I've had to rearrange our schedule and the layout of the tents and categories." The chatter of the crowd fades to a hum as we pass through the thick barn doors, but inside, there's still a buzz, everyone busy with their own tasks and conversations. "The contestants will now come to you and the other judges with their entries. That will save you time and energy. I've found Raylene's replacement, but it's still just three official judges plus Shirley." She points to the row of tables, and my stomach drops.

Helen Cross is seated at the center, her perfectly coiffed hair defying both gravity and humidity. She's holding a clipboard with the kind of authority that makes it look like she might start grading our handwriting at any moment.

Her smile is all teeth and no warmth when she spots me. "Surprised to see me?"

Missy gives me a desperate look. She's on Helen's left. I pull out the chair on my mother-in-law's right and ease into it. "What a relief that you can fill in, Helen. We appreciate your help."

"I hate last-minute invites, but we're family. I didn't want to let Logan down. You know how these things go."

"Sure do," I reply. Mama ushers in a line of contestants, all carrying their sample dishes. "Guess we better get started."

"Now this here," Earl Jenkins says, gesturing proudly to his plate of ribs, "is smoked over pecan wood for eight hours, then glazed with my secret peach bourbon sauce. Family recipe."

I've heard that line with every contestant. I lean in for a closer whiff. "Smells divine, Mr. Jenkins." And it does—the tangy sweetness of peaches mingling with the earthy smoke is enough to make my mouth water.

"Go on, dig in," he urges, practically vibrating with anticipation.

I pick up a rib, careful not to drip sauce on my dress, and take a bite. The meat slides off the bone like butter, and the glaze has just the right amount of kick at the end. "That's... wow," I manage between bites. "You weren't kidding about that glaze."

He puffs up like a rooster in a henhouse. "Told ya!"

"Alright, Earl," Helen cuts in, her pen scratching away on her clipboard. "Let's keep it moving. Lots to taste today."

"Oh, sure." He shoots me a hopeful smile as he slides down to Helen and Missy.

Person after person, dish after dish, I find myself loosening up. The pressure's still on, but somewhere between some cornbread muffins and smoked brisket sliders, I stop worrying so much about getting it "right" and just start enjoying the process. Maybe I really am fine.

Mid-morning, Logan brings me a bottle of water, Moxley wagging along at his feet. "How's it going?"

"Honestly? Not half bad," I tell him. "I mean, I'll need a week to recover from this food coma, but it's kinda fun."

"Hello, son," Helen says, finishing off her notes on a scorecard. "Heard y'all had some excitement over the past few days. Might be nice to call your mother and tell her about it so she doesn't have to hear it from the local gossips."

She's not asking for the scoop; she's demanding first rights. As president of the gossip train, it irks her when she isn't the one to disseminate the juicy stuff first.

Logan good-naturedly leans over and hugs her, kissing her cheek. "You have enough on your shoulders at the winery. Let's schedule dinner for next week, and Ava and I will tell you all about it."

That seems to appease her. He tells me that the silent auction is going great, and that I have over a dozen bids on the Blessings Pie.

I nearly drop my pen. "A dozen? Really?"

Brax calls to him from across the space and he nods at me before he turns to walk away. "Really. I'll be back in a bit."

By the time we reach the last contestant, I've tasted everything from *Phantom Shrimp & Grits* to *Poltergeist Pumpkin Bars*. I can feel my waistband protesting. As I jot down my notes on the final entry—a delicious burnt sugar pudding —I smile. *I did it. I made it through the judging.*

"Thank you, Miss Ava." The final contestant wrings her

hands nervously. "It means the world to us, having you judge today, especially after what happened to Donna."

One of Donna's fans. There are still plenty of them. "I enjoyed it. Thank you for sharing your recipe. You've got something special here."

As I turn in my scorecards to Mama and Shirley, who is using her honorary status to help Mama out, I catch sight of a gauzy figure floating a few feet off the ground near the silent auction table.

Birdie.

She came.

The late afternoon sun dips low over the fairgrounds, casting everything in that golden-hour glow that makes even the rusted hinges on the food trucks look charming. Mama marches up to a small stage set up with a microphone and taps it twice to quiet the crowd. It squeaks in protest, but it does the job. Folks hush, except for a baby somewhere wailing its disapproval of the humidity.

"Alright now, everyone." Mama scans the crowd. "What a day we've had! From barbecue ribs that could make angels weep to the sweetest peach cobbler this side of heaven, I'd say this cookoff has been a rousin' success."

The crowd claps and whoops. I take a moment to soak it all in. The twinkling string lights zigzagging overhead, the laughter bubbling up around me—it's small-town magic at its finest. I glance toward Birdie, but then my eyes land on a familiar figure in a wheelchair off to the side.

Lorna.

She's here, too.

She's smiling and clapping along with everyone else like she hasn't got a care in the world. Her usual frail demeanor has been replaced by something lighter, almost luminous. She's wearing a lavender shawl draped loosely over her shoulders, and for a second, she looks peaceful. Beside her is Shirley.

Seeing Lorna like this makes my chest feel a little less tight. I make a mental note to find her before the night is over. There are some things that need to be said, whether or not I've figured out exactly how to say them.

Mama continues, pulling me back to the moment. "Before we announce the auction winners, let's give a hand to our judges for taking on the Herculean task of sampling every dish presented here today."

A wave of applause rolls through the crowd, and I try to shrink into myself just enough to avoid drawing attention. I'm not great with public praise. It makes my palms sweat. But Logan catches my eye from across the lawn and gives me an exaggerated thumbs-up. Kit and Sage are with him, as are Brax and Rhys, clapping wildly.

Mama clears her throat, the telltale sign she's winding up for the big announcement. "And now, the moment y'all have been waitin' for—the winners of this year's Southern Spirits Cookoff!"

She announces the names and hands out the blue ribbons. There's much excitement and clapping, and even those who come in second and third place are still happy.

"We have one more item," she says. "Because of your generous donations, the silent auction has raised over..." She pauses for effect, and we all hold our breath. "Five thousand, two hundred, and sixty-three dollars for the Birdie Birmingham charity!"

Once the applause dies down, she shuffles her papers

and grins as she eyes the crowd over the top of her reading glasses. "And the winning silent auction item is..."

Again, that pause. My heart beats against my ribs like one of the birds on the recipe cards has come to life inside my chest. I hold my breath. Not because I expect to win, not really, this is Birdie's recipe. Her charity.

"...Ava Fantome-Cross, who submitted Birdie's Blessings Pie!"

Wait. What?

There's a split second where I think I've misheard her. Then the crowd erupts again, those not already on their feet, standing.

"Well, I'll be," I murmur, heat creeping up my neck as I shuffle toward the stage. My hands fumble with the edge of my blouse. I can feel about a hundred pairs of eyes on me, including Helen's, which I imagine are narrowed. I can practically hear her muttering, *Blessings my behind.*

Mama waves me over like I'm a prized hog at the county fair. "Come on up, Ava!"

By the time I climb the three creaky steps to the stage, my shock has melted into something warmer—a flicker of pride. Not for me, for Birdie. For her recipes, her stories, her legacy. This pie *is* more than a dessert. It's a piece of her and her passion.

"Congratulations." Mama hands me a blue ribbon and squeezes my hand. Her smile is softer now, full of that rare mix of love and approval only mothers can pull off. "You made me proud. Birdie, too."

"Thank you," I manage, blinking back the sting of tears in my eyes. "It's—it's an honor. Truly."

And no one better tease me about my cooking again.

The applause swells, and as I glance back at the crowd, I catch Lorna's gaze. She's clapping harder than anyone, her face lit like Christmas morning.

Mama asks me to give a speech. I have no idea what to say and am about to beg off when I catch sight of Birdie again. I step to the mic and go with the truth. "I'm not much of a cook, but I felt the need to honor Birdie and recreate one of her most famous dishes. The entire time I was making the pie, I felt her presence guiding my hands. To the winner of the silent auction, I sure hope you enjoy it and that it does its job—I hope it brings you many blessings."

Another round of applause. Birdie nods at me and vanishes. Mama brings the mic back to her lips. "Let's keep this celebration going! Y'all grab some Conjured Cocktails & Haunted Sips!"

As the crowd disperses to grab drinks at the booths set up with cocktails and mocktails, I step down from the stage, hanging onto the ribbon like it might float away if I loosen my grip. Logan meets me halfway, his grin wide enough to split his face. He wraps an arm around my shoulder. "I knew it would be a hit."

"Yeah, yeah," I reply, though I grin. "You probably bid the highest on it just to save someone else the disappointment of tasting my cooking."

He places his free hand to his chest, indignant. "I did not. But I'd sure love it if you made another for me."

"Only if you don't ask for cinnamon."

He rolls his eyes. "Spoil sport."

I excuse myself to speak to Lorna, grabbing the tin of recipe cards that I've brought with me. The crowd talks and laughs around me, voices blending with the chirp of a few spring field crickets and the faint clink of mason jars. The ribbon in my hand feels heavier than it should—an anchor pulling me toward what I know I need to do.

Lorna's smile is wide, her cheeks flushed pink under the soft glow of string lights. As I approach, her conversation with Shirley drifts into earshot.

"...and wouldn't you know, he brought store-bought potato salad. Store-bought! To a potluck!" Shirley's voice is scandalized. "I nearly fainted right there on the spot."

"Bless his heart," Lorna says, her tone light and teasing. For a moment, I almost turn back. But then I see Birdie again hovering behind Lorna's chair, and I know I can't chicken out now.

"Excuse me, ladies." I plaster on a polite smile as I step closer. "Shirley, would you mind if I steal Lorna for a minute?"

"Well, if it isn't our resident pie queen!" Shirley beams. "Congratulations, Ava. Where on earth did you find Birdie's recipe?"

The back of my neck warms. This won't be easy. "That's what I need to speak to Lorna about."

"Of course, of course." Shirley pats Lorna's arm. "We'll catch up some more later. You behave now, y'hear?" With a wink, she waves at her attendant who rolls her off toward the dessert table.

"She's something, isn't she?" Lorna asks, with a fond chuckle.

"That she is." I glance down at the tin in my hand. "Listen, Lorna, there's something I need to talk to you about. It's important."

Her smile fades, replaced by a flicker of concern. "Is everything alright?"

"Not exactly." I hesitate, searching for the right words. "It's about Birdie."

Her hands clutch the sides of her floral-print cardigan, and her eyes dart to mine, wary and curious all at once. "What about her?"

"Lorna, we... I found her. Birdie, I mean. I found her remains."

For a moment, it's as if the world freezes. Lorna blinks, her mouth parting slightly, but no sound comes out. The color drains from her face, and she sways in her chair enough to make me reach out instinctively, gripping her elbow to steady her.

Her voice trembles. "Are you sure? Are you absolutely sure it's her?"

I nod, my throat tight. "The ME has confirmed it, thanks to the swab you gave Detective Jones with your DNA. And we found this..." I show her the recipe tin. "This was in the cedar trunk with her, but I'm guessing you already know what it is and who placed it there."

Lorna stares at the tin, her fingers twitching as if she wants to reach for it but can't quite bring herself to. Tears well in her eyes, spilling over and tracing lines down her cheeks. "Oh, Birdie." She takes a shuddering breath. "All these years..." Her words tumble over each other as she lifts her gaze to mine. "But how? Where?"

"The trunk was in my attic." I then explain all of it—how Aunt Willa bought the trunk at the estate sale. How it sat in the attic for years until I found it.

Lorna covers her mouth with one hand. Silence ensues.

Then, she grabs the tin of recipes, her knuckles pale and stark against the faded metal.

I don't say a word.

"Chester." The name hisses out between her lips like it's been locked in the back of her throat for decades. "Birdie was gonna run off with Chester."

Am I finally going to get the real story? "Do you know what happened?"

"He was tall, handsome, a real charmer. Birdie adored him." Her lips curl into a bittersweet smile, but it quickly falters. "She told me about their plan the night she planned to leave." Her gaze goes distant, like she's watching the past play out on some invisible stage right in front of us. "They were gonna head to Louisiana, where no one would find them. Said they'd start fresh, open a little diner maybe—Birdie would cook, and Chester would do the heavy liftin'. It sounded like something out of one of those dime-store romance novels she used to hide under her mattress."

My chest feels tight. "But something went wrong?"

"*Everything* went wrong," Lorna sobs, hugging the tin tighter. "I couldn't believe she'd leave me. I hated Chester. Hated him. He didn't deserve to sweep Birdie's kitchen floor, let alone marry her."

Her voice cracks, and she pauses to catch her breath. I reach over and pat her hand again, hoping it'll steady her enough to keep going.

"That night," she says, her tone dropping to a whisper so soft I have to lean in to hear her, "I begged Daddy to stop her. He'd been drinking, and my whining made him angry, but he went to Birdie's. I went with him. I thought he was just gonna talk to her, convince her I needed her. I thought she would stay." Her breath hitches, and tears spill down her cheeks faster than she can wipe them away. "Instead, they got into a fight."

My stomach twists, though I stay quiet.

"She shoved at Daddy to make him move. Her trunk was packed. She wouldn't stay, no matter what. Daddy shoved back, and..."

More tears, more gasps of breath. "Take your time," I murmur.

After a long moment, she gathers herself. "She fell. Hit the back of her head on her stove." Her head shakes as if she's reliving it, her face contorting into grief. "I dropped to my knees, and tried to wake her up, but she didn't. She just... lay there." She trails off, her shoulders slumping forward. "How could she leave me?"

I rub her shoulder. "Was she dead?"

Another deep breath, her frail chest heaving. "Chester showed up."

She stops abruptly, her teeth sinking into her bottom lip like she's trying to physically hold back the words. I wait patiently.

She idly taps the tin with a finger. "Daddy met him in the driveway with a shotgun. Told him to get out of town and never show his face again."

Was Chester dead, too? "Did he? Leave?"

"Nobody said no to Daddy." She breaks down into another fit of sobs, her entire body shaking. "He left, and we never heard from him again. But I didn't say no to Daddy, either."

I sit there in stunned silence. My mind is spinning, and

my heart aches for Birdie, for Chester. Even for Lorna, who's been carrying this awful secret for so long.

She wipes frantically at her tears. Her tissue is soaked. "He made me hide her." Her voice sounds younger. Decades younger. "To clean out the cedar chest and put her in it." She glances at me through her tear-filled eyes. "I didn't want to do it, but I was only seventeen. I was so scared, and I was horrified that Birdie was dead. But Daddy said I had to keep it a secret. That if I told anyone, he'd go to prison. That I would, too. I was so...frightened."

"Of course you were." I want to hug her. "Anyone would've been. You were in an impossible situation, Lorna."

"Doesn't make it okay," she mutters, staring down at the tin. "I should've done right by her. I should've told the truth. My sister didn't even have a proper burial."

We sit in silence for a moment. An idea strikes. "You know, it's not too late." I reach out to take her hand in mine. "I'll make sure Birdie receives a proper burial, okay?"

She looks at me then, her red-rimmed eyes searching mine for something—hope, forgiveness? Maybe both. I squeeze her hand again, silently promising that I'll help her carry this burden, no matter how heavy it may be.

Chapter Twenty-Four

Back at the house, Logan and I take our usual spot in front of the fireplace with a bottle of wine. I'm stuffed to the max, no dinner required.

Moxley flops onto the floor with a dramatic sigh, clearly as worn out as I am. As much as I've been stewing, I have to get Lorna's confession off my chest. "We need to talk."

"That bad, huh?" Logan studies my face. He knows me well enough to recognize when I'm carrying something heavy. And, bless him, he doesn't push. Instead, he tops off my glass, leans back, and waits.

"How do you handle it?" I run my fingers over the stem of the wine glass. "When you know something awful about someone, but telling the truth could ruin them?"

"Well," he starts slowly, as if trying to read my mind. "It depends on the awful thing and the someone. Care to elaborate, or are we speaking hypothetically?"

"Very much not hypothetical." I let out a long breath, then spill it all—Lorna's confession, Birdie's tragic end,

Steven Duval, all of it. By the time I'm done, Logan's leaning forward, having set down his wine glass untouched, his elbows on his knees and his hands clasped together like he's praying for some divine wisdom to descend upon us both.

"Well," he finally says, blowing out a sizable breath, "this is sure a mess. On one hand, you've got an obligation to expose the truth and bring justice to Birdie. On the other hand, Lorna's an old woman who's already spent most of her life haunted by this secret. Reporting her might bring her peace—or it could destroy what little time she has left."

I slump into the cushion. "Don't remind me."

Logan takes my hand. His palm is warm, his grip steady. "Whatever you decide, you're doing it for the right reasons. That counts for something. More than something."

"Yeah, but is it enough?" I stare at our joined hands. "Is it enough to just do my best?"

He squeezes my hand. "Your best is more than most people ever give. Whatever you choose, you won't be choosing alone. I'm here. We'll figure it out."

Sunday morning, the sound of a spoon clinking against porcelain pulls me from my thoughts as I stare out at the backyard. Aunt Willa's rose garden is just starting to really go wild, and I'm grateful for it. Millie Rosemont Bevans is, too. Rosie informed me late last night that the wedding was a success.

When I glance over my shoulder, I find Persephone perched on the counter, one leg crossed over the other as she stirs a glass of tea like she's auditioning for a 1960s Lipton commercial. Her red jumper matches her cherry earrings that bob every time she moves. "What's got your corset in a twist this morning? You won the silent auction yesterday. I thought you'd be happy."

I didn't sleep. My body feels like it weighs two hundred pounds. "I don't know what to do with Lorna's confession."

"Ah, that."

"Yes, that. You knew what happened, didn't you? What she did—or didn't do? What she's lived with all these years?"

She floats down from the counter. "I did."

If only she could have shared that fact and saved us all a lot of time and trouble. "Birdie deserves justice. Folks should know the truth. I promised Lorna I'd give Birdie a proper burial, but everything feels so...tangled."

"Justice." Persephone taps a cherry earring thoughtfully. "Funny thing about that—it's got more shades than a summer sunset. Sometimes it's about rules, and sometimes it's about doing what lets folks sleep easy at night."

"Are you saying I should just let it go?" I narrow my eyes. "I'm not sure I can."

"Not sayin' that at all. I trust you'll figure it out. But as for Lorna..." Persephone's tone softens, her gaze turning wistful. "That woman's carried her guilt longer than anyone should. She made her peace last night when she told you the truth."

"She did?"

"You know I have friends in high places." She gives a sly smile. "From what I've learned, Lorna's lighter now than she's ever been. And Birdie? Oh, honey, she's been waiting on Lorna for years. They're sitting on some celestial porch swing right now, sipping sweet tea and laughing about the good ol' days."

A warmth spreads through my chest at the thought, but it's tinged with sadness. "They're...together now? Actually together?"

"Yes, they're together again. And don't worry—you did right by both of 'em. Now, finish your coffee. You've got a phone call coming in."

The phone rings, sharp and insistent. Persephone gives me a knowing look before vanishing with a shimmer, leaving her tea behind.

I set down my mug and grab the phone. "Hello?"

"Ava? I hope I'm not calling too early."

It takes a moment to place the voice—the president of Birdie's charity, Mrs. Bradley. "Not at all." My stomach drops like a stone. "Is everything okay?"

There's a pause, and then she sighs. "I wanted to let you know that Lorna Duval passed away peacefully early this morning. The nurses said she seemed...happy. At ease. I thought you'd want to know."

My hand tightens around the receiver as a lump rises in my throat. I close my eyes for a beat, aching at the thought of Lorna leaving this world so quietly. "Thank you."

"She didn't have any living family, so the foundation will arrange for her burial. Lorna has a will and a plot. Not with the rest of the Duvals, but in a lovely corner of the cemetery."

"I'm glad. And just so you know, Birdie's remains have been found. Although it's not yet common knowledge, the facts will be released soon. I'd like to pay for her body to be buried next to Lorna, if that's suitable."

"Oh, my. They found Birdie? After all this time?"

"Yes, ma'am. It might be nice to let the sisters rest in peace together."

She pauses and I can almost hear her nodding. "I know Lorna would love that."

"Good." We talk for another minute, getting all the details lined up. After I end the call, I sit at the kitchen table for a moment, staring blankly at the phone in my hand. Relief and sorrow swirl together, leaving me feeling unmoored.

Lorna's gone.

"Well," I murmur to the empty kitchen, "I hope you're at peace now, Birdie. If I'm being honest, I enjoyed having you around."

"I liked it here."

I whip around so fast I nearly knock over my chair. There, standing by the window, is Birdie herself. She looks just as she did in those old photographs—apron and all. Her warm eyes meet mine, and for a moment, neither of us speaks.

"Birdie," I breathe, half-laughing, half-crying. "You're here."

"Just wanted to say thank you. You've got a knack for fixin' things." A pause. "Even the kind of things that usually can't be repaired."

"Does that mean you're okay with how I handled it?"

"Your pie crust still needs work." Her lips curve into a mischievous smile. "But, yes. Don't fret about Lorna. She's got plenty of company where she is."

"I'm happy for both of you."

"Give those recipes to that Raylene gal, will ya? I want my cookbook published."

And I'll buy the first copy. "Of course. It will be a big hit, I'm sure."

Birdie winks, quick and playful, and then—just like Persephone—vanishes. The room feels emptier without her, but also lighter. A weight has been lifted.

Logan comes barreling in and sees me smiling. "What did I miss?"

"I'll tell you over breakfast. Then, I need to talk to Detective Jones."

"Made your decision?"

I toy with the tin of recipes. "You could say that."

He pulls me into a hug. "How about we hit The Honey Bar for breakfast, then tackle Jones on full stomachs?"

Mine is still pretty full from the cookoff. "I have a loaf of Mrs. Davidson's strawberry bread. Family recipe, you know."

He checks the pantry and examines the loaf that the woman wrapped in colored plastic and adorned with a bow. "Didn't she enter her strawberry bread in the contest?"

"She did, after she attempted to bribe me with that very loaf."

He chuckles. "And you accepted her bribe?"

I slap his arm. "Of course not. She gave it to me afterward. I wasn't going to say no then."

"I'm glad you didn't." He starts the coffee maker while I slice several pieces for us. "What are you going to do with Birdie's recipes? Are you finally going to turn them over to Jones?"

"No. I'm giving them to Raylene. Jones won't need them after I give him Lorna's confession, and Birdie told me she wants her cookbook published. She wants Raylene to do it."

"She told you that?"

"Her parting words."

He glances around. "She's gone?"

"She is."

"I think I'm going to miss her."

I plate the bread and grab butter from the fridge. Most things are better with real butter smeared on them. "Me, too," I tell him. "Me, too."

Don't miss the next Confessions of a Closet Medium, Murder & Marigolds, coming in 2026!

Just when Ava Fantome thought Thornhollow's bodies were done appearing in her life, her mama digs up a whole new mess—literally.

During the groundbreaking ceremony for the Ladies Garden Club, Ava strikes more than soil beneath the marigold beds—she unearths a buried body.

Uncovering the decades-old death of Virginia Winthrop's long-lost secretary, she investigates a trail of forbidden love, vanished heirlooms, and encounters a ghostly gardener with unfinished business. But the biggest shock of all? The new club president—prim and proper Marigold Manners—may have a closer connection to all of it than anyone ever imagined.

Secrets grow deep in Thornhollow, and some roots refuse to stay buried.

Stay tuned for *Murder & Marigolds*—a Southern ghost mystery blooming with scandal, secrets, and a garden full of ghosts.

Birdie's Blessings Pie

Passed down with love (and butter) from Birdie Birmingham's kitchen in Thornhollow, Georgia.

Ingredients:

- 1 ¼ cups all-purpose flour
- ½ tsp salt
- ½ cup (1 stick) cold unsalted butter, cut into cubes
- 3 to 4 tbsp ice water
- 5 to 6 fresh peaches, peeled and sliced
- ½ cup granulated sugar (plus extra for sprinkling)
- ¼ cup brown sugar
- 2 tbsp cornstarch
- 1 tbsp lemon juice
- 1 tsp vanilla extract (*optional but highly recommended by Tabitha*)

- Pinch of cinnamon (*optional—but not in Ava's kitchen*)
- 2 tbsp cold butter, diced for dotting
- 1 egg (for egg wash)
- A heaping dose of gratitude and a whisper to the spirits, if inclined

Instructions:

1. **Make the crust:** In a large bowl, whisk together flour and salt. Cut in butter with a pastry cutter (or your fingers) until it resembles coarse crumbs. Add ice water 1 tbsp at a time until dough holds together. Flatten into a disk, wrap in plastic, and chill at least 30 minutes.

2. **Prep the filling:** In another bowl, gently toss peach slices with granulated sugar, brown sugar, cornstarch, lemon juice, vanilla (if using), and cinnamon (if brave). Let sit while you roll the crust.

3. **Roll out the dough:** On a lightly floured surface, roll out the chilled dough and place it in a 9-inch pie plate. Trim and crimp edges.

4. **Assemble:** Pour peach mixture into the crust. Dot with cold butter.

5. **Top it off:** You can add a second crust, lattice, or leave it open. If using a top crust, don't forget to cut vents. Brush with egg wash and sprinkle with sugar.

6. **Bake:** Place pie on a baking sheet. Bake at

375°F (190°C) for 45–50 minutes or until the crust is golden and the filling is bubbling.

7. **Cool & serve:** Let it rest until just warm. Serve with a scoop of vanilla ice cream or a side of gossip.

Note from Birdie: *Blessings are best when shared. And buttered.* 🤍

For more recipes, keep reading, and if grab my Cooking with Ghosts Cookbook!

Cooking With Ghosts: Hauntingly Good Southern Recipes

How This Haunted Cookbook Was Born

If you know me as the author of the *Confessions of a Closet Medium series*, then you already know I spend a lot of time with ghosts.

Fictional ones, of course. (*Mostly.*)

It all started with Ava, my sweet heroine who sees spirits, solves mysteries, and would rather design wedding dresses than talk to the dead—except the ghosts won't leave her alone.

As I was writing her adventures for this story, something funny happened. My ghost characters started bringing *recipes* with them. They'd whisper about peach cobbler secrets, argue over whether cornbread should be sweet (bless their hearts), and insist I write it all down before they vanished again.

One even threatened to haunt my Instant Pot.

That's when the idea hit me—what if the ghosts weren't just part of the story—what if they were part of the kitchen?

And so, ***Cooking with Ghosts*** was born.

This isn't just a cookbook. It's a supernatural supper club, a collection of haunted recipes tied to stories from the other side. Some come straight from Ava's world, while others were inspired by the real-life Southern women in my family—strong, sassy, and not above adding a hex to a ham if someone crossed them.

Whether you're here for the comfort food, the campfire tales, or just curious to see if your great-aunt's fried chicken recipe made it to the other side, you're in good company. Light a candle, tie on your apron, and maybe keep a little salt by the door...just in case.

Because once the spirits start cooking, there's no telling what they'll stir up.

Pull up a chair. It's time for a ghost story and some good cookin'.

Nyx

Grab your copy here:

Cooking With Ghosts

Loretta Belle's Deviled Eggs to Die For

Ingredients:
- 6 large eggs, hard-boiled and peeled
- 3 tbsp mayonnaise
- 1 tsp yellow mustard
- 1 tsp sweet pickle relish
- A dash of hot sauce (Miss Loretta preferred Tabasco)
- Salt & pepper to taste
- Smoked paprika, for garnish
- Optional: 1 extra egg, halved and placed in the center for Miss Loretta

Instructions:
1. Slice eggs lengthwise and scoop yolks into a bowl. Mash with mayo, mustard, relish, and hot sauce. Season with salt and pepper.

2. Spoon or pipe filling back into whites.

3. Dust with smoked paprika and arrange six eggs on a plate. Place the seventh egg half in the center.

4. Serve cold—and don't forget to whisper "Thank you, Loretta."

From Cooking With Ghosts: Hauntingly Good Southern Recipes

Back-from-the-Dead BBQ Ribs

Ingredients:
- 2 racks baby back ribs
- ½ cup brown sugar
- 1 tbsp chili powder
- 1 tbsp paprika
- 1 tsp garlic powder
- 1 tsp black pepper
- 1 tsp salt
- Your favorite BBQ sauce (or the ghost of Miss Tilda will judge)

Instructions:
1. Preheat oven to 300°F (150°C).
2. Mix dry rub ingredients. Rub all over ribs.
3. Wrap tightly in foil and bake for 2.5–3 hours.
4. Unwrap, brush with BBQ sauce, and broil or grill 5–10 minutes.

5. Slice, serve, and try not to drool on your apron. Bones may rearrange themselves.

Modern Tip: Slow cook the ribs with a splash of Coke or root beer, then finish under the broiler for sticky caramelized skin.

For more haunted recipes, check out Cooking With Ghosts: Hauntingly Good Southern Recipes

Cornbread from the Other Side

Ingredients:
- 1 cup cornmeal
- 1 cup flour
- ¼ cup sugar (optional, depending on your stance in the sweet vs. savory war)
- 1 tbsp baking powder
- ½ tsp salt
- 1 cup buttermilk
- 2 eggs
- ¼ cup melted butter
- Bacon grease or butter for skillet

Instructions:

1. Preheat oven to 400°F. Heat a cast iron skillet with a little bacon grease inside.

2. Mix dry ingredients in one bowl, wet in another. Combine.

3. Pour into hot skillet. Bake 20–25 minutes or until golden.

Ghostly Tip: Let a bit of batter drip onto the floor. Old wives say if it disappears, someone else wants a slice.

For more haunted recipes, check out Cooking With Ghosts: Hauntingly Good Southern Recipes

Poltergeist Pumpkin Bars

Ingredients:
- 4 eggs
- 1⅔ cups sugar
- 1 cup oil
- 1 (15 oz) can pumpkin
- 2 cups flour
- 2 tsp baking powder
- 1 tsp baking soda
- 2 tsp cinnamon
- ½ tsp salt

Cream Cheese Frosting:
- 1 (8 oz) cream cheese
- ½ cup butter
- 2 cups powdered sugar
- 1 tsp vanilla

· · ·

Instructions:

1. Beat eggs, sugar, oil, and pumpkin. Stir in dry ingredients.

2. Pour into greased 9x13 pan and bake at 350°F for 25–30 min.

3. Cool, then frost with cream cheese icing.

4. Cut into squares and serve with coffee... or cold dread.

For more haunted recipes, check out Cooking With Ghosts: Hauntingly Good Southern Recipes

Visit My Store

Did you know you can buy directly from me? When you do, the retailer doesn't take a cut and I can pass on the savings to YOU!

https://www.nyxhalliwell.com/books

Benefits:
>You can find ALL my books in one place
>SAVE money
>EARLY access to new releases
>Special Collections and Limited Editions
>Support a small business

Why Buy Direct?
>When you purchase a book by your favorite author, electronic or print, on retailer platforms, the company keeps 30-70% of the sale, leaving the author with little to no profit (after the company deducts delivery fees, taxes, and other fees).

Buying directly from the author means that more goes to them so they can keep turning out stories for you. Every published story, every book, requires cover art, editing, and hours and hours of the author's time simply to create it. Not to mention overhead costs, such as websites, newsletters, writing software, graphics programs, advertising, taxes, etc.

In addition, one of the big-name retailers requires exclusivity, and all of them have terms of service and rules and regulations that make it challenging and time-consuming for an indie author to navigate the publishing world.

Most of us would MUCH rather spend our time creating more stories for YOU, rather than trying to jump through the hoops at the retailers. Buying direct from your favorite authors (where available) helps ensure that an author you love is not subject to unexplained account closures, withholding of royalties, censorship, and other issues that can affect their livelihood.

I've experienced ALL of these. By buying direct, you help put control of my work back in my hands - and I can continue to write more.

Either way, thank you for supporting me! I understand buying direct doesn't work for everyone and even if you use the retailers to buy my books, I appreciate you!

Happy reading,

Nyx

https://www.nyxhalliwell.com/books

Do you love cats, candles, and fun?

Immerse yourself in my cozy world!

Find my books, cozy scented candles, tea mugs, and everything you need to create your perfect cozy reading nook in my shop.

Nyx Cozy Shop

Free shipping on orders over $30. Discount automatically applied at checkout. Spend $100 and get $20 off!

Ready for more magick?

Don't miss the next exciting adventure! Sign up for Nyx's Cozy Clues Mystery Newsletter.

And check out these magical stories:

Sister Witches Of Raven Falls Mystery Series
Sister Witches of Raven Falls Special Collection
Of Potions and Portents
Of Curses and Charms
Of Stars and Spells
Of Spirits and Superstition
Sister Witches of Raven Falls Special Collection

Confessions of a Closet Medium Cozy Mystery Series
Confessions of a Closet Medium Special Collection
Pumpkins & Poltergeists
Magic & Mistletoe

Skeletons & Scandals

Hearts & Haunts
Vows & Vengeance
Cupcakes & Corpses
Tea Leaves & Troubled Spirits
Haunted Honeymoon
Wedding Bells & Psychic Spells
Phantoms Are Forever
Skeletons & Scandals
Cooking With Ghosts: Hauntingly Good Southern Recipes
Murder & Marigolds (Coming Spring 2026)

Confessions of a Closet Medium Cozy Mystery Series Collection

Sister Witches of Story Cove (Formerly Once Upon a Witch) Cozy Mystery Series

Cinder
Belle
Snow
Ruby
Zelle

Sister Witches of Story Cove Complete Set

Witchy Candy Shop Mysteries

Tricks and Treats
Candy and Creeps
Gum and Ghouls

Meet Nyx

USA Today bestselling author Nyx Halliwell loves writing magical stories as much as she loves baking and crafting. She believes cats really can talk (please don't tell her three rescue puppies), and yes, she sees ghosts.

She enjoys binge-watching mystery and paranormal shows with her hubby and reading all types of stories involving magic. She talks to trees, has too many crystals, and drinks far too much tea.

Check out her online store and sign up for her Cozy Corner newsletter at https://www.nyxhalliwell.com.

Dear Magical Reader

Thank you for reading this story! It is an honor and a privilege to write books for you. I'm an indie author and every fan is important to me. I pour my heart into each story and do my best to bring you a delightful escape from the real world.

Readers are the key to my success. Those of you who share my stories with your friends are magic for me.

If you'd like to learn more about my books, sales, and special promotions, please sign up for my newsletter at https://www.nyxhalliwell.com.

Support me directly (no retailer taking their cut), grab special edition box sets, and get new releases before they are out at retailers by visiting my store https://www.nyxhalliwell.com/books. I have sales and offer NEW RELEASES early! Check it out.

Last but not least, if you enjoy grittier, but still fun, urban fantasy, paranormal romance, or romantic suspense, visit my pen name http://www.mistyevansbooks.com to see those books.

Thank you for supporting my dream.

Blessed be,

Nyx 🩶

I have a secret to share with you

A little dream of mine has been growing quietly for a while now, and I'm finally ready to share it with you.

I've been working on a secret project that's especially dear to me—something tender, nostalgic, and full of heart. It's called **Letters From Gram**.

For you

LETTERS OF ENCOURAGEMENT IN YOUR MAILBOX
www.lettersfromgram.com

Growing up, I experienced a profound absence. My

paternal grandmother, Gertrude Anne, passed away when I was only two years old. I'm told she was short like me and had a passion for poetry—sometimes I wonder if my love of writing is a thread connecting us across time.

My maternal grandmother, Eunice, lived far away, and I only saw her once or twice a year before she passed away before my 18th birthday.

I never truly got to know either of them.

Throughout my life, I've felt the absence of that special grandmother relationship—someone I could call when I needed encouragement, someone who would offer wisdom about life's complexities, careers, relationships, and love.

To fill this void, I began writing letters to myself from an imaginary grandmother, creating the nurturing voice I longed to hear.

These personal letters became a source of comfort and guidance during challenging times, and I realized I wasn't alone in this longing. Many of us yearn for a loving family connection—a gentle voice of experience sharing both practical advice and emotional support. Others of us miss those connections after our loved ones have passed on.

That's why I created Letters From Gram. Each letter is crafted with the same care and attention I put into the ones I write for myself, offering a grandmother's wisdom and warmth that so many of us seek, or miss because our own grandmothers have passed on.

My hope is that these letters bring you comfort, joy, and the feeling of connection that comes from knowing someone cares about your journey.

When you receive a Letter From Gram, you're receiving

a piece of the grandmother relationship I've always imagined —and perhaps one you've longed for (or missed), too.

Through Letters From Gram, subscribers receive monthly physical letters, charming notes, and even tiny surprise gifts from Gram and her two cats, Marmalade and Swiftie.

It's a slow moment in a fast world, a cozy hug in an envelope.

• Make going to the mailbox fun again. You'll receive an uplifting letter each month for an entire year.

• Each letter is meticulously written, crafted, and thoughtfully designed by me.

• Each envelope includes a gift from Gram - her favorite recipes, pressed flowers from her garden, charms, tea bags, and more that turn a simple letter into an **enhanced experience.**

• Letters From Gram is a bright spot amongst bad news, bills, and junk mail. Now, you can enjoy a hug, love, and small tokens from a grandmotherly figure.

A dash of old-fashioned wisdom. A sprinkle of kindness. A mailbox full of heart.

Gram's mission, and mine, is to remind you that you're loved, you matter, and someone out there is rooting for you— always. Twelve letters a year will make going to the mailbox fun again and remind you of how important you are in this world.

Because sometimes, what you need most is a hug.

I'd be honored if you'd take a look and let me know what you think. https://lettersfromgram.com

I'm dedicating Letters From Gram to Gertrude Anne and Eunice.

Share this with anyone you think could use a boost. Let's start a movement to bring love and kindness back into our world.

Nyx